Ride
for the Crown

David A. Poulsen

Plains Publishing Inc.

Canadian Cataloguing in Publication Data

Poulsen, David, 1946-
Ride for the crown

Sequel to: The cowboy kid
ISBN 0-920985-17-3

I. Title.

PS8581.093R5 1989   jC813'.54   C89-091O75-8
PZ7.P687Ri 1989

Illustrations by Gundra Kucy
Edited by Nick Voorn

Plains Publishing Inc.
10316 - 121 Street
Edmonton, Alberta
T5N 1K8

Printed and Bound in Canada.

Chapter One

C. J. Findlay was bored. He'd been back at the D Lazy D for almost a week and nothing, well practically nothing, had happened. The previous year when he first came to the little ranch in the foothills, it seemed as if something exciting had happened every day. Yet here he was, entering his sixth day back in Alberta, and he was just plain bored. It was hard to figure.

C. J. rolled back the patchwork quilt and bedspread from his bed, sat up slowly and let his bare feet gently hit the cool linoleum floor. Without moving his feet he stretched across to the big, old oak desk, reached out, grasped his battered copy of Zane Grey's *The Thundering Herd* and fell back onto the bed.

Downstairs he could hear the phone ringing, eventually followed by the sound of a muffled voice – he couldn't tell whose – talking on the phone. He gave it no thought and soon was engrossed in the buffalo-hunting adventures of Grey's hero.

A few minutes later, a voice rang out from below, "Clayton, are you up? Can you come down here please?"

C. J. recognized the voice as that of Aunt Laura.

She was also the only one who hadn't adopted his new nickname, but preferred to call him by his given name. "Sure, Aunt Laura, I'll be down in a minute," he called back.

C. J. bounded out of his bed, placed the book back on its shelf, dressed quickly, ran a comb through his sandy brown hair, straightened the covers on the bed and headed down the stairs.

Everyone was gathered around the kitchen table. C. J.'s rodeo stock contractor uncle, Roy Douglas, was at his customary spot at the head of the table, a cup of steaming coffee cradled in both hands.

C. J.'s twin cousins, Josh and Jenny, were on either side of their dad and were already attacking breakfast. At fourteen, they were the same age as C. J.

Josh waved a cereal spoon and grinned around a mouthful of corn flakes by way of greeting. Jenny, engrossed in reading the cereal box, offered no greeting at all. In fact, she didn't bother to look up.

Josh Douglas was taller, heavier and darker than his cousin. In fact, he was rapidly becoming a smaller version of his father, whom he clearly worshipped.

Roy was a large man, well over six feet tall with a broad, rugged face. He was big all over, especially in the shoulders and chest, and the hands that encircled the coffee cup were huge. Still, though he could when the occasion demanded it be as tough as the broncs he raised, for the most part he was a gentle, soft-spoken, almost shy man.

Jenny was as different from both of them as rain is from snow. She had fiery red hair, which matched her unpredictable temper. While she was as tall as her brother, she was much more slender and angular in build.

C. J. wasn't particularly surprised at her ignoring him this morning. He was used to Jenny's ongoing efforts to display a tough exterior. He knew, as did everyone else in the family, that although she could be outspoken, at times embarrassingly so, inside she was generous and fiercely loyal to the members of her family and to the ranch she loved.

Aunt Laura, a small woman with auburn hair and a round, kind face, was at the stove pouring herself a cup of coffee.

"Gee, I must've slept in," C. J. started to apologize.

"Not really, C. J. We were up extra early this morning," said Roy Douglas, waving his big hand casually.

"We were expecting an important call," Josh added.

"We got it, too," Jenny chimed in, her eyes still riveted on her bowl of Cream of Wheat.

"Would you like some breakfast, Clayton?" Aunt Laura asked her nephew, with a congenial gesture of welcome towards the table.

"Yes, ma'am, thank you; those corn flakes will be just fine," he replied, taking a seat, his eyes never leaving the plate of hot baking powder biscuits on the table.

Almost as if it had been rehearsed, three hands reached out and instantly the biscuit plate was empty. For a second C. J.'s eyes registered his surprise but he quickly recovered. By the end of the previous summer he had become accustomed to the Douglas sense of humour and love of practical jokes, and he laughed aloud at this latest prank. The Douglases joined in and soon C. J. was enjoying cereal, juice *and* biscuits.

He hastily consumed one of the biscuits before asking, "What was the phone call all about?"

Roy Douglas hesitated, then put his coffee cup down. He looked seriously at his nephew.

"I'm afraid...," he began, then cleared his throat. "I'm afraid you're going to have to go back to Toronto earlier than expected, C. J."

"Whaaat?" came the blurted response. "Why? I thought I was going to be rodeoing all summer with Josh and Jenny. Dad even told me I could stay till Christmas if I made the Canadian Finals. He couldn't have changed his mind. He just couldn't have!" The boy's voice was practically a wail.

To make matters worse, it didn't appear that anybody, other than C. J., was very concerned about the situation. In fact, it looked as if his cousins were having a difficult time keeping from laughing out loud. "What is going on here, anyway?" C. J. demanded looking from one to the other of the faces that were all looking back at him. "Aunt Laura, won't you tell me what's happening?"

"Would you like more biscuits, Clayton?" his aunt asked in her sweetest voice, the corners of her mouth turned up in a mischievous smile.

"All right, that's enough," Roy Douglas laughed, "I think it's time we let C. J. in on our secret."

"I agree," C. J. nodded vigorously.

"Well, what we told you is partly true," the boy's uncle began. "The fact is, we're all going to Toronto. The Douglas Rodeo Company has been hired to put on a rodeo in Maple Leaf Gardens."

"Wow!" whooped C. J. "When?"

"Right after the Calgary Stampede's over," Josh put in.

"Just think," Jenny slapped the kitchen table to emphasize her point, "first the Calgary Stampede and then Maple Leaf Gardens in Toronto...what a summer!"

C. J. leaped up from the table. "Come on," he urged his cousins into action, "I've got to start getting Doc Holliday ready. I want him looking extra great for this trip... we can take him along, can't we Uncle Roy? I know we don't normally, but . . . well, it *is* Toronto, and just think how good he'd look in Maple Leaf Gardens."

"With *you* on his back," Jenny said pointedly.

"Well... uh... yeah," C. J. admitted in a soft voice.

"Let's see," Roy Douglas rubbed the side of his jaw. "He should be finished breeding the mares by then . . . and you might just have a point. A black stallion would look pretty good at that, if he was well-groomed of course."

C. J. had heard enough. He bolted out the kitchen door, hardly hearing the calls of his cousins, "Hey, what's the hurry, it's two months before we leave for Toronto." But it was too late. C. J. was already halfway to the corral that housed the magnificent horse he'd been "given" by Uncle Roy the summer before.

Doc Holliday had for years been one of the toughest broncs on the rodeo circuit, throwing off, at one time or another, every big-name cowboy that had ever climbed on him, including – back in his riding days – Roy Douglas.

The previous summer Doc had been near death from the dreaded horse disease, colic, and had been nursed back to health by C. J., who had refused to leave the stricken horse's side. Since then, the two had formed a remarkable bond: a wild stallion and the only person who could ride him, a boy from eastern Canada.

The corral was one of the most picturesque spots on the whole ranch. It was adjacent to a small, bright red barn that housed only Doc Holliday, Jenny's Barrel Racing horse, Sugar, Josh's chestnut Scooter and a nineteen-year-old mare that had been the "learning" horse for several young would-be riders, the most recent C. J. himself.

The corral and barn were situated on a piece of high ground on the D Lazy D. To the west, the foothills occupied the foreground.

Behind them, looking like a painting, the peaks of the Rockies rose in the early morning haze. It was spring and there was still plenty of snow capping the jagged, blue slopes of the shimmering mountains.

Reaching the corral, C. J. perched himself on the top rail. He began telling his equine companion in great detail about Toronto, Maple Leaf Gardens and all of his Toronto friends who would be surprised and envious to see the boy they knew as Clayton riding at the rodeo on the back of a spectacular black horse. C. J. was in the process of describing the C. N. Tower to Doc when Josh and Jenny approached the corral. "Gee, too bad you couldn't get a little excited about heading out east," Jenny teased.

"Yeah, I know how much you're going to hate having to go out there, but... well, you'll just have to tough it," Josh added with a grin.

"Just think," C. J.'s eyes were glistening in the early morning light, "Maple Leaf Gardens! And we'll be there, all of us: you, me, Doc, my Mom and Dad... it's going to be the best time of my entire life!"

"Yeah, well it won't be so great if you fall off your steer in front of your parents and all your friends," Josh's voice became serious. "We better get practicing; how about we run in a few right now?"

"You bet!" C. J. replied and with a final rub of Doc Holliday's neck, he jumped down from the corral fence to head for the practice pen with Josh and Jenny.

Josh had been riding steers for four years and C. J. had started during that eventful summer the year before. This year both boys were intent on making the Canadian Finals, which meant that they would have to be among the top six Boys Steer Riders in Canada for the entire season. Josh had qualified the year before and had got off to a fast start for this rodeo season, but for both boys to fulfill the cowboy's dream and make the finals would take a lot of work ... and a little luck.

They were about halfway to the practice pen when they saw it. At first they weren't sure what it was, but all three were convinced that what they were looking at was, without a doubt, the strangest sight they had ever seen.

Approaching slowly from the north pasture, about one quarter of a mile away, was the sorriest-looking horse in Canada, maybe North America. And on the back of the sway-backed, bony-ribbed, sleepy-eyed cayuse was an equally odd-looking pair of riders.

In front rode Hector Levy, the D Lazy D's resident hermit whose primitive cabin, all he owned in the world, was saved from a prairie fire the year before, by the efforts of the Douglases and their neighbors.

Hector was doing a better than passable impersonation of Ichabod Crane as his skinny, bearded, unkempt figure bobbed up and down on the plodding animal beneath him.

Behind Hector was a boy. He was a young boy, by all appearances, whose tidy blond hair and scrubbed-cheek appearance contrasted with that of his chauffeur. Strangest of all though was the boy's clothing. He looked completely out of place in the Alberta foothills. In fact, he looked as if he had just stepped out of a picture from somewhere in the Alps.

As Jenny was to comment later, he resembled, if such a person were to exist, Heidi's brother.

The arrival of this bizarre-looking pair put the steer riding plans on hold and C. J., Josh and Jenny stood wide-eyed and open-mouthed as the apparition drew nearer.

Chapter Two

It took the slow-moving horse what seemed like forever to cross the final fifty metres separating the two groups but at last Hector, the oddly-dressed boy and the woeful-looking animal thudded to a halt directly in front of the three onlookers.

Ordinarily a sight like this one would have sent all of them, and particularly Jenny, into fits of laughter, but on this occasion their surprise stunned them into disbelieving silence.

"Boy needs a place to stay," Hector Levy jerked a thumb to indicate the young man seated behind him. "Been stayin' with me the last couple of days. Needs a better place than mine to stay at."

Josh and Jenny knew Hector well enough to know that what he had just said constituted a long speech for the shy, reclusive man. They also knew they weren't likely to get much more information out of him.

Josh stepped forward and offered to help the young boy down from the back of the horse. The boy took his arm and jumped lightly down to the ground.

There was a long moment of concentrated staring from everyone. The newcomer looked from one to the other of the three teenagers in front of him. They looked back at him. He was shorter and slighter than the others and looked to be a couple of years younger. His hair was extremely blond, almost white, and provided a vivid contrast to his darkly tanned face and light-blue eyes.

He seemed fascinated by their attire. All three were wearing, as usual, cowboy boots and stetson hats, blue jeans and checkered western shirts. Josh and Jenny sported large fancy buckles on their belts, trophies of past rodeos, and it was on these that the newcomer's gaze seemed particularly fixed.

Jenny spoke first. "What's your name, anyway?"

The boy offered no reply, but looked over at Hector who had been staring steadfastly at the ground. The hermit looked up at Jenny, "I never thought to ask him," he shrugged.

"Where's he come from?" Josh directed his question at Hector.

Hector shrugged again, "Germany or somethin' I reckon," he replied vaguely. "Well, I best be off."

With that, he turned his horse slowly around and began easing his way back in the direction he had come.

"Wait a minute," Josh called. "You aren't serious about leaving him here, are you? I mean, just like that!"

Hector, in his maddeningly slow fashion, turned the horse yet again, returned to the group of youngsters and spat a tobacco chew on the ground. "You're right. I'm forgettin' somethin'." He pulled a knapsack from the back of the saddle and tossed it to Josh. "This belongs to him," he said, pointing to the boy. "There's a coupla shirts in there, another pair of them short pants he wears, some socks and a sandwich I made him in case you weren't home."

Having said that, Hector turned his horse and slowly began retracing his path one more time.

"Hector, where did you get that horse," Jenny blurted, unable to contain herself any longer.

"Traded for 'im," the hermit called back. "What d'ya think of 'im? Traded a guitar and an old plow for 'im. I call 'im Shakespeare."

When the spectacle of the horse and rider was out of earshot, C. J. said, "I bet he calls him Shakespeare because he's poetry in motion."

The laughter of the trio was interrupted by the final words of Hector Levy, called back from far off.

"By the way, there's fifteen hundred dollars in that knapsack. Belongs to the kid." Then Hector disappeared up and over a hill, without seeing the shock registered on the faces of the twins and C. J.

Josh reacted first to this new information. He passed the knapsack to C. J., who passed it to Jenny, who returned it to a very reluctant Josh.

"I can take that if you wish," the small boy told them.

"Hey, he can talk!" Jenny exclaimed.

"He can speak English!" C. J. added in the same tone.

"In that case," Josh said, as he gingerly handed

over the battered satchel to its rightful owner, "maybe you better tell us who you are and what you're doing here."

"My name is Rudolph Kruger. I don't suppose that name means anything to you, does it?" The boy's very proper but somewhat accented voice sounded strangely anxious.

" 'Fraid not," Josh replied. "Your name doesn't ring a bell. Where you from?"

At that the newcomer seemed to relax and said, "I live in Switzerland actually. I'm... uh... holidaying here in Canada for the summer."

"Your accent," Jenny interjected, "it doesn't sound... uh...."

"German?" Rudolph helped her out. "I suppose it's not, though I speak the language fluently. But I've been going to school in England, which explains my accent.

"Well, there you are, now you know everything about me. I don't suppose we might eat something. While I appreciate Mr. Levy's valiant attempt at a sandwich, I really could use a... "

"Hold on a minute," Josh interrupted him firmly, "what do you mean we know everything about you? We don't know anything about you. For instance, how you got here... what you're doing... and where you got a knapsack full of money."

Rudolph laughed a nervous, high-pitched kind of laugh.

"I can assure you I am not a burglar, if that's what

you're worried about," he explained with a careless wave of his hand. "Actually I have been vacationing in Canada with my father. Unfortunately, in the middle of our holiday in Banff he was called back to Lucerne on urgent business.

"I'm quite used to being on my own, so Father consented to let me continue alone. I'm to meet up with him in a few weeks. I must say he would probably be a bit surprised at my mode of travel."

He cast a glance over his shoulder in the direction where Hector Levy had disappeared with his horse. "I was hitchhiking when I met Mr. Levy."

"You mean your dad lets you travel around Canada by yourself?" Jenny sounded amazed.

"Indeed yes, why not?" came the reply. "And by the way, the money in the satchel is my travelling allowance. Actually there's only a little over fourteen hundred dollars in there, but if I should run out, I can have more wired to me at any Canadian chartered bank.

"So you see, you have nothing to worry about, now do you? I really would like something to eat now, if it wouldn't be any trouble."

"No... no trouble... I guess," Josh mumbled, still baffled by the bizarre arrival of this strange boy and his equally strange story.

"You talk different. Where'd you learn to talk so... smart?" Jenny asked.

"Smart?" repeated Rudolph. "I suppose I do speak English rather more correctly than... some people. I would think it comes partly from my English boarding school education and partly from the fact that I read rather a lot."

"Oh yeah, well we read too, Mr. Smarty Pants," Jenny replied indignantly.

"I'm sure you do," Rudolph acknowledged with a patient smile. "Actually I was thinking of something in more of a classical vein: Shakespeare, Thomas Hardy, D. H. Laurence, Dickens... "

"Ah ha," C. J. interrupted triumphantly, "we're reading a book of Dickens right now in class... *Great Expectations.*"

"Ah, and what do you think of Pip and Magwitch, Miss Havisham and the lot?" asked Rudolph, his interest picking up.

"Uh... I guess we haven't got that far yet," C. J. admitted ruefully.

"And how far are you?" inquired Rudolph.

"Well, we're just at the part where the boy meets the convict in the graveyard," Jenny explained.

"I believe that's chapter one, if I remember correctly," Rudolph surmised.

"Yeah, I know," C. J. glumly nodded.

"Come on, we'll take you up to the house," Josh led the way.

"It should be fun explaining this one to Mom and Dad," Jenny said to no one in particular, shaking her head in bewilderment.

There was no one in the kitchen when the four youngsters made their silent entrance into the house.

Josh and Rudolph sat at the now vacant kitchen table, while C. J. and Jenny busied themselves rounding up some breakfast fare for their guest. Not wanting to seem snoopy, no one asked any more questions of the new arrival, at least until he was partway through a bowl of strawberries and cream and had started on his second biscuit.

"What are your plans anyway?" C. J. asked Rudolph after he and his cousins had explained to the boy how the ranch operated and about the family's involvement in rodeo.

"Plans?" Rudolph repeated slowly while he heaped a generous mound of butter on to half of a biscuit. "I don't know what my plans are really... other than to see some of Canada and...." He shrugged to indicate that his plans were no more definite than that.

"What do you call those pants anyway?" Jenny asked, a pained expression on her face. "You look like something out of *Sound of Music*."

"These are called lederhosen," Rudolph grinned in reply. "They are very popular in my part of the world. I take it you don't like them."

"Are you kidding?" the red-haired, freckled teenager replied. "Those are the worst, the ugliest, the...."

At that moment, Roy and Laura Douglas came up from the basement, their arms full of old newspapers and magazines.

They were accompanied by a sleepy-eyed, yellow dog who, on seeing the group in the kitchen, came to life. He eagerly made the rounds with much panting and tail-wagging. Casey, the family pet, offered a slightly less enthusiastic welcome for Rudolph, who in turn reached down and scratched behind the dog's ears.

"What would spring be without spring cleaning?" Laura Douglas' voice could be heard behind the stack of newspapers she was struggling with.

Josh and C. J. sprang to her aid and the newspapers were deposited in a large pile near the back door.

"It'll be you kids' job to burn 'em in the burning barrel," Roy Douglas said as he dropped the last of his load onto the pile.

Then, as he turned around, he finally noticed the young stranger sitting at the table.

"Whoa, now who is this?" Roy asked, stopping in his tracks.

"I didn't hear any cars arrive," Laura Douglas noted, looking around for more strangers.

"There's a good reason for that Mom," Jenny explained with a sideways glance at Rudolph.

And with that began the explanation of Rudolph's strange arrival and the repeating of his story for the rest of the Douglas family.

As Rudolph completed his story, which had been interspersed with comments and nods of agreement from Josh, Jenny and C. J., Roy and Laura Douglas exchanged glances.

Roy Douglas took a deep breath. "We're accustomed to extending a welcome to anybody who comes to our door, son," he addressed Rudolph, "but to tell you the truth, I'm having a little trouble believing your story. Now if you've run away from home or if you're in trouble, it would be better if you told me now, so we can let your parents know where you are. They're probably worried about you."

Rudolph rose abruptly from his chair. "I assure you, Sir, that such is not the case. The truth is exactly as I have relayed to you. I am in no trouble and if you find it inconvenient to extend to me the hospitality of your home... "

The boy stopped in mid-sentence. Outside the sound of a light aircraft could be heard, coming closer and closer.

The Douglases and C. J., used to the sound of crop-spraying planes and rodeo cowboys flying low overhead to "buzz" their friends below, paid little attention to the sound.

But as the aircraft roared directly over the ranch house just a few hundred feet in the air, the face of Rudolph Kruger contorted in panic and before anybody could stop him, the boy dived head-first under the kitchen table!

Chapter Three

As the family members recovered from their initial shock at the newcomer's strange behavior, Roy and Laura Douglas lifted the table cloth and looked underneath. Rudolph was curled up in a ball with his arms covering his head.

Laura Douglas broke the silence, "Are you all right, Rudolph?"

The boy slowly lowered his arms and looked up. The look of fright on his youthful features slowly changed to sheepishness. He stood up and surveyed the concerned faces that were gathered around him.

"I guess I owe you all an explanation," he began. "You see ... when I was very young ... about five, I think, yes I'm sure I was five, my father and I had a very close call while flying from Vienna to Zurich. Ever since that time, aircraft have frightened me, even the sound of them nearby. I'm dreadfully sorry if I've caused you to be alarmed."

"No need to apologize, son," Roy Douglas told him, "but I'm afraid we're going to have to check your story out. I'm not calling you a liar, Rudolph, but I have trouble buying that a boy your age would be left running around a foreign country on his own."

"Please Mr. Douglas," Rudolph's voice lost its self-assured quality, "you must believe me, please, I promise you ... I give you my word that I have not run away from my parents.

"I know it sounds a little strange that I'm on my own but I can even show you my return airplane ticket."

The boy fumbled in the frayed knapsack and in a minute pulled from it a tattered but official-looking folder with BEA written across the front. He handed the folder to Roy Douglas.

Roy and Laura Douglas examined the contents of it carefully.

Finally Laura Douglas said, "It certainly looks official all right. One ticket on British European

Airways from Toronto to Heathrow, London, and a connecting flight to Vienna, Austria," she read from the tickets.

"I have to admit it looks official to me," Roy Douglas said, rubbing his chin thoughtfully.

"Hey, *we're* going to Toronto!" Jenny enthused.

"When?" Rudolph's eyes lit up.

"In late July," Josh explained, "right after the Calgary Stampede."

"But that's perfect, don't you see?" Rudolph beamed triumphantly. "I have to be back at school August first."

"That seems to be true," Laura Douglas mused, still examining the airline tickets. "His flight is scheduled for July 26."

"Oh Mr. Douglas, this is wonderful. If you could let me stay, I'd be happy to pay you for your trouble and then, if I could travel to Toronto with you, I'd be so grateful. Oh please, Mr. Douglas."

"Rudolph, I'm not about to give you any commitments for two months. For now you can stay the night and we'll talk about it some more tomorrow." Roy was frowning as he spoke.

"And another thing ... we won't be accepting any of your money. This isn't a hotel, it's a ranch and if you do stay... mind you I'm saying if, then you'll have to work around here just like everybody else."

"But I'd love to do that," Rudolph's eyes were aglow with delight. "Just think, me, a cowboy; that would certainly shock everyone at home."

"I can relate to that," C. J. acknowledged.

"Well, we've got just the way to get you started, cowboy," Josh told him. "We were just about to ride some steers. You can come and give us a hand."

"Wonderful, let's go!" Rudolph shouted happily.

"I'll be there in a minute," Jenny called over her shoulder as she started for the telephone, "I want to phone Cindy and tell her the news. She'll faint when she hears there's somebody here from Austria!"

"Excuse me, Jenny," Rudolph's voice stopped her. "You wouldn't mind dropping this somewhere out of the way for me, would you?" he asked, handing her the knapsack.

Jenny's freckled face went white. "You mean, you want me to hold on to... fifteen... fifteen hundred dollars?" she gasped, taking the satchel like one would pick up a skunk.

"Of course, why not?" Rudolph laughed as he fell in behind C. J. and Josh who were already headed for the practice arena.

"By the way fellows," he called as he hurried after the cousins, "what sort of saddle shall we use for riding these animals?"

It was a couple of hours later and the sweat was pouring from the faces of Josh and C. J. Each had ridden four steers so far and another was in the chute awaiting Josh to take his last turn.

The steer riding practice area was a small circular pen with an eight-foot-high plank fence all around.

Two home-made chutes were located at the east side of the pen. Behind them was an area for keeping the steers prior to loading them into the chutes for their turn in the little arena.

The practice pen received a little shelter from a small stand of poplars on its north and west sides but at this time of day the sun beat down unabatedly on the riders and their helpers.

Jenny had been opening the bucking chute gate for the two steer riders while Rudolph perched on the nearby fence and shouted encouragement and kept track of eight seconds, the length of a regulation rodeo ride. At the end of each eight second ride he shouted "time," in a voice that Jenny claimed could be heard in Calgary. At that point the rider threw one leg over the steer and fell to the ground on one side of the animal.

Josh had ridden all four of his steers in relatively easy fashion while C. J. had ridden three and bucked off one tougher-than-average steer at about the six-second mark. This delighted Jenny who heaped good-natured scorn at the embarrassed cowboy.

Josh climbed up and over the chute gate and began the preparations for his upcoming ride. He began by "warming" his rope, the process of rubbing his gloved hand up and down the tail-end of his bull rope which was already looped around the girth of the steer.

C. J. held the end of the rope to allow Josh to rub resin into the rope, thus warming the resin and making it stickier.

Josh then inserted his hands into the handhold of the rope. After getting his hands into a comfortable position, he signalled C. J. to begin pulling the rope tight.

As C. J. snugged the rope up, he passed it down into Josh's open palms, then around behind the rider's wrists and into his hands a final time.

Now Josh clamped his hands as tightly shut as he could make them around the tight rope. He then slid up the steer's back to sit as close as possible to his hands and nodded his head.

Jenny, watching alertly for her brother's signal, released the latch and swung the gate open.

As soon as the steer saw the open gate, it burst from the chute and into action. In fact, though, the steer was of the mediocre variety. It bucked straight away and without much power, allowing Josh once again to easily go the required eight seconds aboard the animal.

As Rudolph's shrill voice once again pealed the eight-second signal, Josh dismounted almost casually from the back of the Hereford steer and, loosening his chaps, made his way back to the chutes.

Other than the seemingly never-ending chatter of Rudolph and the occasional sarcastic jibe from Jenny, conversation was at a minimum.

The two riders themselves rarely spoke, going about the business of preparing and riding in stony-faced, almost grim seriousness. Occasionally, Josh offered a word of advice to his cousin, which the eastern boy usually accepted with a nod.

Another steer was run into the chute, this one a stocky, tawny brown Simmental, and the two boys reversed their roles of the previous ride. It was C. J.'s turn. As a less experienced rider, he still underwent an occasional bout of apprehension which he tried hard not to show.

All of the steers had been hand-picked by Roy Douglas for their docile manner in the chutes and this one was no different.

Had the animals been at all wild, Roy would have been there to assist the boys getting on, just as he usually was at a rodeo where the stock was generally much tougher than these practice steers.

The steer stood calmly while C. J. took his final wrap, slid up on his rope and nodded. The gate opened and the ride was underway.

The steer offered a little more challenge than Josh's had, but C. J. had things under control and was making a good ride. At virtually the exact second that Rudolph yelled "time!" the steer — for no apparent reason — seemed to lose its footing.

The animal stumbled almost to its knees, then recovered, righted itself and jumped high to buck again.

The timing of the incident couldn't have been worse. C. J. was loosening his hold on his bull rope in preparation for his "get-off." In that position, the boy was virtually defenseless and totally unprepared for the sudden power unleashed by the steer that had been startled by its near-fall.

When the steer came down again, C. J. was

dangerously tipped to the right and as the animal's front feet hit the ground hard, the helpless rider was whipped around and down on the back of his head.

The sickening thud of C. J.'s brutally hard landing was plainly audible over the warning "look out!" shouted by Josh.

In an instant Josh was beside his fallen cousin. Jenny got there just a fraction of a second later.

C. J. had remained motionless since the impact.

"He's out," Josh told his sister. "Run to the house for Mom and Dad." Jenny flew into action, scampering over the fence and racing for the house.

Josh didn't know what to do. He was aware that it was dangerous to try to move C. J. but felt he should do something. C. J. looked badly hurt.

All the color had completely drained from the injured boy's face, his eyes had rolled back in his head and there was a frightening gurgling sound coming from his throat.

Josh knew instinctively that C. J. was in serious trouble. If only he knew something about first aid! If only Mom and Dad were here, they'd know what to do. Suddenly Josh felt himself being pushed aside.

"Out of the way, quickly! Let me at him."

The command came from Rudolph, who had been completely forgotten during the sudden crisis.

"What are you doing?" Josh shouted, and in a naturally protective reaction, pushed the smaller boy away.

Rudolph faced him, his boyish face now grim.

"Look, I've had some training. If you don't let me look at him ... he could die. He's not breathing!" He was shouting the words.

Josh looked quickly back at the stricken C. J. Rudolph was right! C. J.'s chest, that seconds before had been heaving desperately in an apparent effort to get air, was still.

"Help him," Josh whispered numbly, scrambling back out of the way. "Help him if you can."

Quickly, Rudolph ripped open the top buttons on C. J.'s shirt and bent over to peer intently into his face.

"I need something...," he told Josh, without looking up, "something long and narrow ... a stick ... something...." He cast a desperate look around.

Josh jumped up. "I'll run to the house!" he shouted.

"There's not enough time," Rudolph told him. "Wait! That! Give me that ... your spur," he pointed, "and hurry!"

Josh swiftly pulled the spur from his boot and handed it to Rudolph. "I have to hold his head back like this," Rudolph quickly explained. "He's swallowed his tongue, and if I don't get it out, he'll suffocate," he told Josh.

Again he bent over C. J.'s unconscious body. The gurgling in C. J.'s throat had diminished to an occasional gasp-like sound. Rudolph carefully wedged the rowelled end of the spur into one side of C. J.'s mouth and delicately probed. Twice he tried to position the spur under the tongue that was securely lodged in C. J.'s throat and twice he failed.

The third try he was able to force the rowel under the tongue in the hope of using it like a lever to pull the tongue back into its correct position. Delicately he pulled back on the spur and almost had it when it slipped and C. J.'s tongue slid back into his throat again.

Patiently but quickly Rudolph went back at it again, probing, inching the spur further into C. J.'s throat, positioning.

All the while he was talking, as if to coach his own movements. "Now pull ... gently, bring it up, don't lose it. Don't let your hand tremble even a little."

And there it was! He'd done it. C. J.'s tongue was out of his throat and back up into his mouth.

"Way to go!" Josh breathed a sigh of relief.

"We're not done yet," Rudolph told him, "I've got to start him breathing again."

He bent over C. J. again, pinched the young cowboy's nostrils shut, and began to apply mouth-to-mouth resuscitation, first breathing much-needed air into C. J.'s mouth, then pausing to watch his chest.

Behind him Jenny, Roy and Laura Douglas were hurrying over the corral fence but Rudolph was unaware of their arrival, so intense was his concentration on the critical procedure he was performing.

Roy ran quickly to where C. J. lay. "Let me take ov..." he began, reaching down to pull Rudolph out of the way.

He was stopped in his tracks by a silent gesture from Josh and a gentle pressure on his arm from his wife. "I think he knows what he's doing," she said quietly.

After what seemed an eternity, C. J.'s chest weakly heaved, once at first, then again, this time a little stronger.

Slowly the boy's breathing was being restored and though it was, at first, a little erratic, he was breathing nevertheless. C. J. was going to be all right.

Josh looked up at his father, mother and sister. There were tears in his eyes.

"You know something," he said in a voice cracking with emotion as he looked back at Rudolph, "he just saved C. J.'s life."

Chapter Four

It was several minutes before C. J. regained consciousness, slowly opening his hazy eyes.

For another half hour he was not allowed to move. His first attempts to speak were unsuccessful, the result of what had taken place in his throat a short time before.

It was frustrating for C. J. There were things to say, questions to ask and yet each attempted word wound up as not much more than a raspy squeak.

When he was finally able to talk again he couldn't remember anything that had taken place since the arrival at the practice pen. Eventually he was able to sit up, still weak but regaining some of the color in his face. As he continued to recover, Josh related to him and the others how Rudolph's quick thinking and instant reaction probably had saved him from suffering worse damage or even death.

"Looks like we owe you quite a debt of gratitude," Roy Douglas told Rudolph, who was now lying back resting on his elbows next to C. J.

"Where in the world could a boy of eleven years have learned all that?" Laura asked him, making no effort to hide her amazement.

"Actually, I'm a trainer for our school's football team in England, although I've already learned that what we call football, you call soccer," Rudolph chuckled. "The truth is, I've taken several courses to qualify me as an athletic trainer."

He lowered his voice confidentially, "I must tell you, though, this is the first time I have ever been put to the test."

"You mean you've never had to work on anybody before?" Jenny was dumbfounded.

"Never," Rudolph grinned at her nonchalantly. "At least not for anything more serious than having one's breath knocked out or the odd minor sprain."

"Boy, for your first case, 'doctor', you sure did a fine job," Josh told him. "I thought you must have done this sort of stuff lots of times before."

"Well, every doctor needs a first case, doesn't he?" Rudolph returned, then looked at Jenny.

"Boy, first he's a scholar; now he's a medical whiz," Jenny chipped in. "Yep, a regular sawbones."

"And whatever is a 'Sawbones' may I ask?" Rudolph said cheerfully.

"A sawbones ... well now, that is just a country nickname for a doctor," Jenny replied.

"Come to think of it, I think maybe sawbones'd be a better name to call you anyway," she mused. "I'm having trouble getting used to Rudolph."

"I think I prefer Rud..." Rudolph began, then stopped in mid-sentence looking thoughtful.

"Actually," he continued, "I think 'Sawbones' is a

fine nickname, and you're welcome to refer to me as that anytime you wish," he beamed at her.

"We want you to know that we're very grateful for what you did," Laura Douglas said seriously.

"That's right, son, "Roy added, "we won't soon forget it."

Rudolph looked at him earnestly. "In that event," he spoke slowly, "do you think it would be possible for you to trust me and let me stay? It's only for two months and I promise I won't be any trouble to you and then I'll be on an aircraft heading for home and you won't ever have to think about me again and..."

"Hold on there," Roy interrupted him, laughing, "I think I understand what you're saying. I'll tell you what I'll do." Roy looked around and saw that every eye was directed at him and every face looked hopeful. "I need a little time to think about this, but I promise I won't do anything until after Cloverdale."

Rudolph looked puzzled.

"Cloverdale's our next rodeo," Jenny explained. "It's right outside of Vancouver. It's one of the best rodeos anywhere; you'll just love it."

"We're leaving the day after tomorrow. We'll be gone for almost a week," Josh added.

"You mean I can come along, Mr. Douglas?" Rudolph's face lit up.

Roy smiled at him and said, "I think we can find room for one more, don't you?" He looked at his wife.

"I'll just throw a little more water in the soup pot," Laura Douglas winked. Josh, Jenny and Rudolph whooped in celebration while C. J. showed his approval with a tired, silent grin.

"Well, I think it's time we got rolling," Roy restored order. "I'll go up and get the pickup and we'll run C. J. into the hospital in High River."

"Aww, do I have to?" C. J. groaned.

"Sure do, son," Roy ordered, "and my guess is they'll pronounce you as good as new and we'll all be able to get started getting ready for Cloverdale. We've got a long trip ahead of us."

"There's just one thing I can't figure out," C. J. said rubbing a hand over his lips. "I have this terrible taste in my mouth."

Rudolph reached down and retrieved Josh's spur from the ground and handed it back to its owner.

"That's odd," he said, "I wonder what that could be from."

The loud laughter that followed was mostly the result of the great relief all of them felt.

The preparations for Cloverdale began the next day. By 6 a.m., the D Lazy D was a beehive of activity. Ben Bradley, pickup man for Douglas Rodeos, and retired competitor Len Tucker, whose desire to win the All Round Championship of Canada had nearly cost him his freedom the summer before, were at the ranch early to help the Douglas family get ready for the journey and the rodeo.

Roy Douglas, Len Tucker and Josh were hard at work sorting the bucking horses and bulls that would make the trip. C. J., who had been released from hospital after a couple of hours of observation and a warning to "take it easy", was working alongside Ben Bradley. They were busy performing last-minute maintenance on the vehicles, including the huge stock liners, that would make the convoy to the coast.

Closer to the house, Laura Douglas supervised a team made up of Jenny and Rudolph. Their job was to load the motor home with the provisions necessary to keep the travellers fed and clothed during the seven days they would be away.

Jenny, never one to miss an opportunity, was relentless in her good-natured abuse of the hapless "Sawbones," who, as the newest member of the D Lazy D team, was "low man on the totem pole."

Rudolph, however, was having such a good time assisting the family in getting ready for the trip, he barely noticed the teasing and bossing. A perpetual grin creased his youthful features.

"C'mon, hurry up eh! Get those sleeping bags loaded, will you?" Jenny urged.

"Aye aye captain," came the cheerful reply.

It seemed the merrier Rudolph was in accepting her treatment of him, the more exasperated Jenny got. "Hey Sawbones, what's the matter with you anyway?" she mocked. "Don't you know anything? The towels go in the cupboard above the sink; the canned goods go under."

"Right you are, then," he sang back to her, "towels up, cans down ... got it."

At noon all three work parties gathered at the

house for lunch and to recap what they had done.

"Stock's pretty well sorted," Roy Douglas said as he poured out lemonade for the thirsty workers.

"This afternoon we'll ride up and get that band of mares out of the north pasture. There's three of them I want to take to Cloverdale and the rest'll be turned out with Doc Holliday for the next couple of months," he explained. "How's it going with the vehicles?"

"All right, Roy," Ben Bradley replied. "We're gonna have to replace a seal on the manifold on the Kenworth. Got a bit of an oil leak. Otherwise everything's ready to roll."

It was Jenny's turn to report.

"Well, we'd be finished by now if I didn't have to follow along behind Mr. Klutz here," she gestured at Rudolph, "and redo everything for him."

Rudolph and C. J. winked at one another.

"It's sure great having a new kid around here," Josh grinned broadly. "At least it keeps my sister out of our hair, right C. J.?"

"That's for sure," C. J. replied, his voice no longer showing any signs of his recent ordeal.

Jenny was about to set the two of them straight when she was interrupted on two fronts.

Laura Douglas emerged from the kitchen with a steaming pot of stew at exactly the same moment a maroon three-quarter-ton truck with a tack box on the back pulled into the driveway and came to a stop not far from the house.

It was McKannin's truck. Mr. McKannin was at

the wheel. He'd driven over to drop off Cindy who would be making the trip to Cloverdale with the Douglas entourage.

"Oh no," Jenny groaned. "Look out everybody, C. J. could swoon and end up falling right into the stew."

C. J. took the gibe without offering a response. It was, after all, true that he and Cindy had hit it off rather well the summer before. It was also true that Jenny and even Josh could be merciless in their teasing.

"Just in time, Harold," Roy called. "Come on over and dig into some stew. There's corn bread here too."

"No thanks, Roy," came the reply. "We ate before we came, but I do need to talk to you for a minute."

Harold McKannin looked serious as he stepped up on the porch. Behind him, Cindy's face showed none of its normal cheeriness.

"What's up, Harold?" Roy asked, pulling up a pair of chairs for the new arrivals.

"Well," Mr. McKannin said, a hand over his chin, "I might be wrong but..."

"You weren't wrong, Dad, I saw them too," Cindy stated firmly.

"What was it you two saw?" Roy Douglas was beginning to look concerned.

"As we were coming over here," Mr. McKannin began again, "we saw a black pickup up on the hill straight east of your place. There were two fellas alongside of it."

"They didn't appear to see us coming and we got pretty close to them," he went on. "It looked for all the world like they were watching your place with binoculars.

"When they finally did see us, they jumped in their truck and high-tailed it...," Mr. McKannin accepted the glass of lemonade Mrs. Douglas held out to him.

"... but not before we got a good look at them," he continued.

"It was the Shivers boys!" Cindy pronounced the words venomously.

Silence struck the group. Lefty Shivers and his

younger brother Miles had become archenemies of the D Lazy D the year before, when they had used vicious and dangerous tactics in an effort to sabotage the Douglas rodeo operation and eventually take it over. Everyone on the ranch had hoped they had seen the last of the evil pair with the end of the previous rodeo season.

"Those rotten skunks!" Jenny exploded.

"I can't believe they'd come anywhere near this place ever again," Josh uttered the thought that everyone shared.

"Who are the Shivers boys?" Rudolph asked, looking around at the hills that surrounded the ranch.

"Two of the worst, no-good, rotten to-the-core, no account, disgusting..." Jenny was getting warmed up.

"Let's just say they're two characters that rodeo could do without," Laura Douglas clarified for Rudolph.

"The entire planet could do without those two!" Jenny spat the words.

A sense of dread descended over the group. No one spoke for a while as each retreated to his or her own thoughts. Surely, the Shivers boys wouldn't dare to try anything further at the D Lazy D, not after their previous efforts had been so unsuccessful.

And yet, they had obviously been spying on the ranch. One thing was for sure ... if the Shivers boys were up to something, everyone on the ranch would have to be very careful in the days and weeks ahead.

Chapter Five

By the following morning everyone's spirits had improved as the excitement of the impending trip overcame their suspicions and concerns of the previous evening.

Still, extra caution was taken in checking the vehicles to ensure that no tampering had been done.

"You can't be too careful when the Shivers boys are around," Jenny explained to Rudolph.

"This is one time my sister is right," Josh agreed, "I don't know what their game is but I'd be willing to bet they're up to no good."

C. J., too, had run up against Lefty and Miles Shivers the previous year and was quick to voice his own dislike for the brothers.

"You couldn't find a worse pair of... of... " he began. "Jerks," Jenny supplied the word in her typically direct fashion.

"Jerks," C. J. concurred vigorously. "All the same, I can't believe they'd want to mess with the D Lazy D after the lesson we taught them last year."

The threesome was soon engaged in a recap of how they had finally got the best of the Shivers boys the year before. The account was punctuated with gales of laughter and the occasional burst of anger.

Throughout the conversation and, in fact, ever since Mr. MacKannin and Cindy had reported what they had seen the night before, Rudolph had been almost completely silent. Even his ever-present grin was gone.

Cindy was first to notice.

"What's wrong, Rudolph?" she inquired. "You sure are quiet lately."

"Really? Do you think so?" Rudolph shrugged his small shoulders and worked up a half-smile. "I guess I'm just not used to cowboys and bad guys yet. I thought that only happened in the cinema."

"Well, no need to be scared," Jenny told him confidently. "Mom and Dad are pretty good at looking after us and Dad has a couple of pretty tough hombres working for him.

"I don't think the Shivers boys would want to mess with Ben Bradley or Len Tucker." She held up a fist to indicate what she meant.

It was obvious that if Rudolph wasn't frightened, he was at least preoccupied. He spent much of his time gazing around at the hills and paid particular attention to the main road that passed about a half-mile to the east of the D Lazy D.

"You expecting someone, Rudolph?" Josh finally asked him.

"Expecting someone? Me? No, no, of course not." The reply was a little too hurried.

"If there's anything you feel like talking about, we

don't mind listening," Jenny said, her softer side coming to the surface.

For a minute, it looked as if Rudolph was about to say something. But just as he appeared ready to speak, a loud blast from a truck horn signalled that the caravan was about to get underway.

All five youngsters scrambled to take their pre-assigned places. In the first liner, which was now loaded with broncs, Ben Bradley would be at the wheel with C. J. riding alongside.

Josh would ride with his dad in the next liner, now loaded with bulls.

Next in the caravan was the ranch's pickup truck pulling a home-made trailer loaded with equipment for the rodeo. Len Tucker and Rudolph would be the crew for this vehicle.

Bringing up the rear was the Douglas motorhome with Laura Douglas driving and Jenny and Cindy in the passenger seat. Behind them was the two-horse trailer with Sugar and Cindy's horse Catfish aboard.

Placing all the females in one vehicle wasn't the result of any male-oriented tendency on the part of the D Lazy D male element. It was due more to the fact that Laura Douglas was the only one who could tolerate the non-stop chatter of the two girls, particularly when the topic of conversation got around to both girls' favorite subject – barrel racing.

Neither C. J. nor Rudolph had ever travelled extensively through the Rockies; in fact, neither had been west of the Banff townsite. Yet, the reaction of each to the unfolding landscape was very different.

For C. J. the soaring peaks provided ample reason for continuous neck-craning and a never-ending series of "oohs," "aahs" and the occasional "awesome!"

Rudolph, travelling in the vehicle behind C. J., was certainly interested in the undeniably spectacular scenery, but his interest was almost school-like. He compared this peak or that one to the ones he was familiar with in the Alps. It was obvious he had spent a great deal of time in and around mountains. While his observations were never the "oh, they simply can't compare with our mountains" kind, they were far less awe-inspired than those of C. J. who was much more the tourist.

Both, however, shared a love for the mountains and carried on a running conversation on the CB radios. From the time the caravan left Banff and moved west through Lake Louise and into British Columbia, the CB microphones were rarely out of the two boys' hands.

The long descent down the Field hill, one of the steepest inclines in the Rocky Mountain highway system, provided a few hair-raising moments for the travellers, particularly those in the semi-trailer units.

The voice of Roy Douglas crackled over the radio to let the others know that there would be a fuel and lunch stop at the bottom of the hill in the little town of Field.

After the vehicles were fuelled, the travellers gathered in a service station restaurant. Three tables were pulled together to accommodate the entourage, and almost instantly the excited voices of the teenage travellers filled a corner of the restaurant.

"Did you see where that avalanche had come down?"

"Weren't the Three Sisters fantastic?"

"Didn't that mountain with all the snow make you want to be skiing?"

The pace and tone of the conversation dropped only slightly with the arrival of the food. The result was that lunch took longer than Roy Douglas had anticipated and by the time they had all finished, he was impatient to be underway.

Once again the travellers arranged themselves in their respective vehicles and began the part of the trip that promised to be the most spectacular and perhaps the most dangerous.

From Field to Revelstoke, a distance of about two hundred kilometres, the Trans-Canada Highway would become a series of climbs and descents, hairpin turns and, in places, embankments of some several hundred metres. It was no trip for the faint-hearted and each member of the Douglas Rodeo outfit felt an inner twinge of anticipation.

These roads hadn't been designed for semi-trailer loads of livestock and the next few hours would surely be difficult ones.

That thought didn't deter the younger members of the entourage and quickly the CB radios in all of the vehicles were humming once again.

This time, Josh in the second liner and Jenny and Cindy at the "backdoor" joined in as well. Normally, Roy Douglas didn't allow the CB's to be tied up for this sort of activity but in this stretch of the Rockies there were unlikely to be many other users on the radio.

Still, he insisted that the youngsters employ a seldom-used channel of the radio. He also stipulated that every ten minutes they get off the air for a while to allow anyone else requiring the use of the radio to get on the air.

"Well, here we are, gang! We have officially entered the Rogers Pass," Josh announced as they passed the entrance to the famous stretch of highway.

"Can you imagine what it must have been like to build a railway and a highway through these mountains?" Jenny chirped.

"An engineering marvel, to be sure," Rudolph agreed.

For mile after mile, one stupendous scene was surpassed by another of still greater beauty.

"Did you see that?" breathed Cindy from the rear vehicle.

"You mean that needle-shaped peak?" the voice of Josh Douglas came back.

Even the adults were having trouble containing themselves.

"Hey, you guys, take a look at those two mountain sheep up there on that ridge!" Ben Bradley shouted from behind the wheel of one of the big rigs.

"Hey yourself, pay attention to the road," Len Tucker kidded him.

"There's two more up a little higher," Cindy noted.

Suddenly, and without warning, the light mood and relaxed atmosphere of the travellers were shattered. The horrified voice of Josh Douglas burst over the radio, "Look out back there! Rock slide ... a big one ... coming down on our right!"

Instantly, gears ground, drivers slammed gas pedals to the floor and the two semi-trailers careened through a narrow channel in the pass.

At the back of the caravan, Laura Douglas was far enough behind the others that by slamming on the brakes she could avert moving into the path of the swift-moving destruction.

But directly in the path of the slide, with no chance to escape either ahead or behind, were Len Tucker and Rudolph in the pickup. Above them, several tons of rock and boulders plummeted mercilessly down the mountainside.

From the lead truck, Josh looked back and screamed a desperate warning into the CB. "Look out! Look out!"

Then, as an ear-splitting roar filled the entire mountain pass, the truck, trailer and two occupants disappeared beneath a cloud of dust and flying rock!

Chapter Six

The roar that had seconds before been so deafening was now replaced by an eerie silence that settled over the entire mountain valley. For several seconds, the rest of the Douglas rodeo crew looked on in shocked silence. Their bodies numb, no one moved; no one spoke.

As the first shock passed, they began to mobilize.

Roy Douglas, now unable to see past the huge pile of shale and rubble that covered the highway, spoke into the microphone, "Laura, are you all right back there, come on ... Laura, can you hear me, are you by?"

"Roy, yes I'm here," the stunned voice of Laura Douglas replied. "We're all okay back here, but I'm afraid Len... and Rudolph..."

Her transmission ended in a muffled sob.

"I know, I saw," Roy forced his voice not to break.

"Listen, Laura, do you think you can turn the motor home around?" he asked her. "I want you to go back. About six or seven miles up the road there was a Highways Construction camp.

"Tell them we need every man and piece of equipment as fast as they can get here. Can you do that?"

"Yes, I think I can. We'll have to take the horse trailer off but I'm sure we'll be able to get back to that camp," Laura Douglas replied.

"Right, I'll get C. J. on the emergency channel on the CB and he can keep radioing for help," Roy added. "We'll start digging here. Away you go now. Good luck!"

"Roy, do you think...?" Laura began the question that was in all their minds.

Roy Douglas couldn't bring himself to answer, at least not within earshot of the younger members of the family.

"Away you go now," he repeated, "and take care."

The remaining members of the team swung into action.

"C. J., you stay on the radio here in the truck. Just keep calling for help."

He pulled open a map. "I'd say our position is about twelve miles east of where the Illecillewaet River intersects the highway. Anybody who can come with equipment, tell 'em to get here fast."

C. J. nodded to show his understanding of the instructions.

"If you get the R.C.M.P. on there, tell them where we are and what's happened." Roy began moving toward the ominous looking hill of rubble on the highway. "And when you've done that, come and help us, we'll need every pair of hands we can get," he called back to C. J. who was climbing into the cab of the truck.

With that Roy was off on the run, a hurried arm signal bringing Josh and Ben Bradley with him.

"We've got two problems, I figure," Roy told the two as they sprinted towards the slide. "First, the rocks may have crushed them. We'll have to be careful when removing the rocks not to make things worse and cause another slide." Then he added, "Our second problem is that we have to move fast. There's no telling how much air is trapped in there ... maybe not much. If they're still alive, we've got to get to them fast if we're going to save them."

They were at the edge of the pile.

"All right, easy now," Roy cautioned. "Let's get up on top and start moving this stuff. Josh, you start moving small pieces and throw them well clear. Ben, you and I can handle the bigger rocks for now."

"There's a lot of these boulders we won't be able to move without some heavy machinery, Roy," Ben pointed out.

"I know," Roy acknowledged, "but let's move what we can for now until we can get some equipment here." They reached the crest of the rubble pile and were surprised to see Laura Douglas, Jenny and Cindy climbing up from the other side.

"Some elderly people came along in a small car so we sent them back," Laura explained.

"Besides, we wanted to help here," she said firmly.

This wasn't the first time Roy Douglas had encountered the stubborn courage of his wife and knew that no argument would prevail.

Silently the group of six attacked the murderous rocks with grim, unspoken resolve. The work went slowly, but as they worked the band of rescuers grew in number. Motorists, most of them vacationers, joined in willingly in an attempt to save the pair trapped below.

C. J. arrived, having reached the R.C.M.P. on the radio and, like the others, threw himself into the tortuous task without a word.

An hour passed, and few words had been exchanged. Despite the workers' feverish efforts, the pile had diminished but little.

Suddenly Ben Bradley shouted, "Hey, help is here! Here comes the heavy equipment."

Sure enough, approaching fast from the east side of the slide was an army of trucks, bulldozers, graders, tractors and men. At the head of the procession, a short, stockily built man with reddish hair and beard jumped out of a pickup truck and ran forward.

"I'm the foreman of this outfit; they call me McCormack," he told Roy in a business-like voice.

Roy briefly explained the situation.

Quickly the dynamic McCormack took charge. "You get your people on the west side there and start working towards us," he told Roy. He turned back to where his own crew was busy peeling off jackets, donning hard hats and distributing picks and shovels. "Get those dozers unloaded," he shouted. "You men start on that corner there."

It was obvious that this crew had had plenty of

experience with rockslides. Not a moment was wasted; not a move was without purpose. In minutes the Highways crew was making a fair-size dent on the east side of the slide. On the west side, cowboys and motorists, men and women took heart from the arrival of the professional crew and renewed their attack on the rocks, boulders and rubble.

For two hours the work continued at an unbelievable pace. Men, women and even children whose bodies ached and whose clothes were soaked with sweat took only momentary pauses to gulp air into burning lungs or grab a quick drink of water. Then they hurled themselves once again at the destructive hill.

In the west, the sun was beginning to sink lower in the sky warning of the impending darkness. The task would surely be twice as difficult in the dark, even though lanterns and spotlights were being set up.

Two ambulances, three R.C.M.P. cars and a television crew had joined the growing cast of characters that had become part of the unfolding drama.

Overhead, a helicopter hovered, ready to rush anyone seriously injured to hospital.

McCormack seemed to be everywhere, now yelling instructions, now shouting encouragement. His pace was twice that of even the hardest worker and the confidence he displayed let everyone know that if anyone was capable of leading them successfully to Len and Rudolph, McCormack was that person.

He and a small crew of men were working from the top of the pile. They were creating a hole in the centre of the pile so that digging was actually taking place on three fronts.

Suddenly, McCormack began shouting in the most frenzied kind of way and waving his arms as if he were trying to fight off a swarm of bees. He ran down from the pile, waved even more frantically at the equipment operators, then rushed back to the top once more. At first, no one could understand what the fiery Irishman was up to, but as machinery was shut off and people stopped working, it became possible to hear what McCormack was saying.

"I heard something," he yelled excitedly. "I think I heard someone yelling!"

The exhausted band from the D Lazy D scrambled gingerly to where the rescue foreman was now on his hands and knees, ear pressed to the surface of the rocks. They dropped to their knees around him and adopted the same posture, each straining to hear some sound from the rocks below.

There it was! It was faint but clear.

"Help!" came a voice from below. It sounded like it was coming from a cave far in the distance.

"Can... you... hear... me?" came the halting call again.

McCormack pressed his mouth to a break in the rocks.

"I can hear you," McCormack shouted in reply. "Are you all right?"

"... okay," the distant reply came back as the first words were unintelligible.

"Say again," McCormack called down. "Are you all right?"

"I ... am ... okay ... having ... trouble ... breathing," was the laboured response.

"That's Len!" Roy Douglas announced excitedly. "Ask him if Rudolph is all right."

McCormack bent forward again "Is Rudolph all right?" he called down.

"He's ... fine ... we're ... both ... fine," Len's voice could faintly be heard.

A cheer went up from the rescuers. McCormack signalled again for quiet.

"We'll be there soon," he called down to the trapped pair. "We're very close to you now. Don't try to call to us anymore. Conserve your oxygen."

He straightened up and with one nod set the rescue process back in motion. The rescuers, both professional and amateur, encouraged by the knowledge that the objects of the hunt were alive and well, overcame their exhaustion and attacked the rocks like they were an enemy that had to be conquered ... and conquered *now*.

Within an hour, another thunderous cheer went up. As the sun's final rays were descending on the dramatic scene, the rescue party at last sighted the roof of the pickup. It was sitting upright with the driver's side door nearest the hole the rescuers had been digging. The hole was a little to the side of the truck.

McCormack cautioned the rescuers. "We can't get careless now. A wrong move could delay getting them out and could even get them badly hurt. We'll go straight down from here and end up right alongside the driver's side door. That way we lessen the chance of bringing more rocks down on the truck itself."

With almost exasperating care the last rocks were eased from their places and passed from hand to hand on to the bucket of a waiting bulldozer.

"I can see them!" Ben Bradley whooped a few minutes later. "Len's got his usual grin on his face and Rudolph just waved at me."

Still, McCormack refused to allow caution to be thrown to the wind.

"Easy now, easy," he repeated over and over.

At last the window on the driver's side was clear of the rocks. A kind of miniature tunnel led down the final few feet to the window of the pickup.

"Any chance we could get some food sent down," Len called up. "This window's jammed and I can't get it down more than a few inches."

"I can get down there easy," Josh told McCormack.

"I know you can, son," McCormack replied," but we can't risk it. We can't take a chance of causing even a small slide now that they're exposed."

"Sorry," he called down to Len. "It's too risky. We'll have you out of there in no time."

For a moment, the spirits of the group gathered around the rock mound sagged. To be this close and realize they couldn't get the trapped man and boy out of the truck without more digging was a bitter disappointment.

"Could you hurry up, please?" Rudolph's voice suddenly piped up. It sounded a little desperate. "I don't mind having to wait for food but I'd really like to go to the bathroom."

"Oh no," Jenny wailed. "We're on national television and he's talking about going to the bathroom."

The roar of laughter that followed was just what was needed to restore the spirits of the weary rescuers.

"All right, let's go," McCormack's voice once again sounded the battle cry. Now they were working in the shadowy semi-dark of the early sundown hours. Still, steady progress was made as the job now was to enlarge the existing hole. In what seemed like no time, McCormack called a halt to the digging and ordered everyone but Roy Douglas back.

"This part's risky," he explained, "but I might need a hand. You game to stay up here?"

"You bet!" came the reply.

"I guessed that would be your answer," McCormack flashed his easy grin, then went right back to work.

"Bring that dozer forward," he barked an order.

The bulldozer operator eased the huge machine ahead with the bucket raised, until the massive tracks were just inches from the steep east face of the slide.

The bucket was perched directly over the hole

leading down to the partially uncovered truck. Quickly McCormack fashioned a large strap which he then hung from the bucket like an oversized belt.

Next, the rescue foreman surveyed the hole closely once more.

Then he knelt beside the hole to call instructions to the anxious pair below. "All right, we're ready," he spoke calmly and carefully.

"Now ease the door open as gently as you can and don't step out of the truck until I tell you."

Len Tucker was plainly visible inside the truck. He tried the door gingerly. Then again. And a third time.

"It won't budge," he called up to Roy Douglas and McCormack. "It must be jammed as well from the slide."

"Don't force it," McCormack warned Len. He turned back to his men. "Bring up those railway ties. We're going to have to brace it."

Quickly the highways men unloaded the ties and brought them one at a time to the top of the mound. Soon a pile of the six-feet-long, eight-inch square ties was stacked neatly next to the hole.

"Okay, I'm going to have to go down there," McCormack announced. "Once I'm down, lower the ties down one at a time with the bucket."

"Wait a minute, I can go down," Roy told the rugged foreman.

"You can, but you won't," McCormack grinned at him. "That's what they pay me for."

Without another word he twisted himself into the

leather strap and signalled to the caterpillar operator to lower him slowly. When McCormack reached the bottom in the hole, he detached himself from the strap and ordered it to be pulled back up.

Roy Douglas shook his head at the courage of the little man who now stood unprotected in the middle of a hill of rock that, if it caved in, would crush and kill him in a split second.

Working steadily and with no sign of fear, McCormack detached each of the ties from the strap as it was lowered into the hole. He then manoeuvered the heavy blocks onto their ends and pressed them up against the wall of rock. Soon he had a layer of the ties in place around the lower half of the hole except for an opening at the truck's door. Quickly he fastened the ties one to another with metal plates and screws. He feared that the pounding of hammer and nails could bring down the rock walls around him.

Then as he worked from the bottom of the hole and Roy Douglas from the top, they repeated the process, creating a second layer above the first that extended to within six inches of the top.

At last McCormack gave the signal that he was to be brought out. For an hour and a quarter he had been in terrible danger, yet the look on his face as he came out of the hole was that of a man pleased with doing a good day's work.

"Well," he called back down to Len Tucker and Rudolph, "I think that should hold it. Now you can be a little more forceful with that door."

Len nodded and went to work trying to open the stubborn door. Still he had no luck.

"I'm going to have to really give it a good shot," he shouted through the crack in the window. "Think she'll hold?"

McCormack bent down and surveyed the makeshift bracing one final time. "I believe it will," he nodded gravely, knowing that if he was wrong the violent smash on the door of the truck could result in its occupants being trapped again ... or worse.

Len Tucker moved Rudolph well over onto the passenger side of the truck. Then he rolled onto his back and drove the door as hard as he could with both legs.

Len was a strong cowboy who had been in shape all his life but the door, though it groaned and creaked, refused to budge.

He froze and listened for the telltale rumble that would indicate that a cave-in was about to occur. There was no sound. "Whew," he whispered at Rudolph. "This is getting a little hairy, you know what I mean?"

He laughed weakly as a nervous sweat spread over his heavily-tanned brow. "Looks like your handy work is going to hold together." He gave the thumbs-up signal to McCormack up above.

"Once more and I think that door should give," McCormack returned the victory gesture.

Again, Len Tucker rolled onto his back and gathered every ounce of his strength to deliver a violent two-footed kick to the stubborn door. It sprung open! But, that noise, that rumbling – was the bracing giving way? The rocks were straining to break through the barrier as the movement of the truck shook the slide.

"Come on, move it!" McCormack shouted, realizing that speed was all that could save them now. "It's not going to hold long."

"Lower that strap," he barked to the operator of the bulldozer.

Len Tucker reached back and grabbed Rudolph and practically threw him from the truck and into the strap that was now in the hole.

The boy lifted himself into the strap and grabbed hold. Gently the belt was raised. As Rudolph reached the top, Roy Douglas grabbed the boy and passed him to a highway crewman who hustled him out of the danger area.

The rumbling was louder and now Roy and McCormack could feel the rocks moving beneath their feet.

Again the strap was lowered – closer and closer to the waiting Len Tucker.

The rumbling grew still louder. "Grab it! Hurry up! It's all coming down!" McCormack screamed the words.

Len Tucker leaped, grabbed the strap and at that instant the caterpillar operator jerked the bucket up and backed up at the same time. The result was Len flying through the air attached to the strap like a fish on a hook.

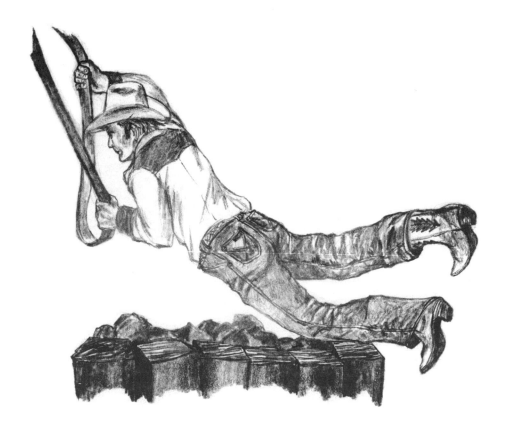

The slide was caving into the hole. The last two people on the hill were Roy Douglas and McCormack.

McCormack grabbed the arm of the bigger man and yelled, "Jump!"

Chapter Seven

The two men hit the side of the slide and scrambled to keep their balance. Behind them the cave-in had made kindling of the huge railroad ties, and the hole where seconds before Len Tucker had been, was gone.

The pickup truck was once again buried beneath tons of rock and shale.

Murray McCormack and Roy Douglas lost their bid to keep their feet as they tried to run and slide down the last face of the huge rock pile. It didn't work. Both men found themselves bouncing off rocks and rolling down the hill, completely out of control. They came to the bottom where rough hands were waiting to keep them from being thrown hard to the highway's pavement.

For several seconds neither man tried to get up. Instead, each gingerly moved first this limb, then that to ensure that all of their respective parts were still in working order.

Ambulance attendants had rushed to their sides and were giving them a check-over before letting them get up.

Roy Douglas had a bad gash on his forehead right at the hair line. The checkered shirt he had been wearing was now hanging in shreds on his bruised, dust-covered body. He pushed the attendants aside and struggled to his feet.

"Where's Len? Did he get out of there all right?" he questioned looking around to get his bearings.

"Up here, Roy," came the cheerful reply.

Len, with no time to get into a sitting position in the leather strap, had simply grabbed hold with both arms. Had he not been able to maintain his hold when the cat operator jerked him from the hole, there is no doubt he would have been crushed in the ensuing cave-in.

Now, however, he had pulled himself up to be sitting in the strap and was perched there with a bird's eye view of what had followed, including the close call of Roy and McCormack.

Len grinned at his employer and friend, "Boss, I don't know how to tell you this, but I think the pickup's gonna need a paint job."

Roy Douglas, brushing aside the blood that was dripping down his forehead, couldn't help but laugh at the comment. Trust Len to be able to find humor in a situation that moments before had threatened their lives.

"McCormack, how about you ... you okay?" Roy turned his attention to the gritty little Irishman.

A few feet away from where Roy had come to rest, the rescue boss was getting to his feet with the help of two of the medical people.

"I was doin' fine until I bounced off that boulder

right there," McCormack pointed at a jagged rock about a third of the way from the bottom of the slope.

"It's his shoulder or his collarbone," a doctor explained as he continued to examine the foreman. "I'd say a break most likely. We'll have to run him to the hospital in Golden for X-rays."

McCormack turned to one of his men. "I'm putting you in charge, Knowles; it looks like I'm going to have go with these people.

"It's just a simple matter of getting the highway cleared now." McCormack's face was a mixture of pain and angry disappointment. It was evident he wanted to stay to see the job completed. Even he knew, however, that a one-armed foreman would be ineffective and he allowed himself to be guided toward one of the waiting ambulances.

Roy walked over and blocked his path.

"McCormack, you saved some lives here tonight," he told him. "We're mighty grateful. If you ever happen to be in the country southwest of Calgary, there's a ranch down there that'd be proud to have you as a visitor."

McCormack looked up at the man who stood a head taller than himself.

His words were formal and seemed odd coming from this fiery man whose energy, courage and stamina had been the difference between defeat and triumph.

"I'd be honored to have the opportunity to visit you and your family at your ranch someday," he said, his eyes glistening in the illuminated night.

With that he walked slowly to the ambulance and, without looking back again, climbed in.

Roy Douglas had one more person to check on. As he received relieved embraces from his wife and children, he looked around again.

"Where's Rudolph?" he asked, alarm registering in his voice.

"Well, dear...," Laura Douglas began trying to suppress a smile.

"You won't believe it Dad," Jenny smacked her palm to her forehead in disbelief. "First he wouldn't even talk to anybody until after he'd gone to the bathroom. And then he said that with all these people around he wanted to look his best and he's gone and put those stupid short pants on again."

"Lederhosen," corrected Josh.

"Those stupid lederhosen," Jenny grumbled. "He's going to look ridiculous on T.V. dressed like that."

Then, as she began to realize how weird it all was – how close they had come to losing two of their friends, and how one of those friends was about to make a T.V. appearance in a pair of funny Bavarian pants – she began to laugh.

They all joined in the laughter loud and long. However, Rudolph took so long to change that by the time he had come back, the television crew, faced with a deadline, had packed up all their equipment so that they could leave as soon as the road was cleared.

When he discovered that he wouldn't be appearing on television after all, the boy looked relieved. Jenny for her part breathed a sigh of relief that they wouldn't be disgraced by Rolf's short pants.

The laughter began again, and Rudolph realized that while he was the object of the outburst, it was as much out of joy as it was the result of his choice of trousers. He joined in as loud and as long as anyone.

For a long time it seemed as if many of the volunteer rescuers were reluctant to be on their way.

It was obvious that a bond had formed between the travellers who had pitched in to help and were now covered with sweat and dirt, and the rodeo family they had stood beside in the all-out effort to get to Len and Rudolph.

Each came by to say his own personal good-bye to Roy and Laura Douglas and to shake hands with Len and Rudolph who, in turn, thanked everyone.

Eventually the time came to leave. A lane had been cleared on the highway and vehicles were permitted to pass.

The bone-tired rescuers climbed into their vehicles and, with a final wave, began the next leg of a journey that had been unexpectedly dramatic.

Roy gathered his family and hired men together to plan some strategy.

"We've got a rodeo to put on starting the day after tomorrow, and we're going to put it on despite what happened here," he announced resolutely.

There were nods of agreement from everyone.

"Now, we've got a few problems," he told them. "All of our flanks, chaps, saddles and flags for the

Grand Entry are buried in the pickup. We'll have to get replacements on the way. Tonight we'll stop in Revelstoke. We'll unload the stock at the stockyards and feed and water 'em before we check into a motel. Tomorrow morning the liners can load up again and continue to Cloverdale.

"Len, I'd like you to travel in the motorhome with Laura and the girls. The Buchanan Brothers Stock Contracting Outfit's headquartered about an hour's drive north of Kamloops.

"Take a detour up there and borrow or rent everything we'll need. Anybody have any questions?" Roy asked.

"What about the pickup?" Len inquired. "We tried to get under a ledge when we saw the slide coming. It might still be worth something." The look on his face was doubtful even as he spoke the words.

"We'll collect what's left of it on the way back through," Roy replied. "I'd at least like to salvage some of our equipment out of the back. Anything else?"

The weary band in front of him shook their heads as one.

"Okay, let's head out. I think we could all use a little rest," Roy told them.

"Oh and by the way, I want to thank all of you for all that you did today. You were all fantastic." he said softly.

"That goes double for me," the ever-cheerful voice of Len Tucker echoed.

"Me too" added Rudolph with a tired attempt at a grin.

The group dispersed and made their way to the vehicles. On the way Josh waited until they were out of earshot of the others, then took hold of his dad's arm and pulled him aside.

"Dad, there's something I want to talk to you about," he began, looking around to ensure that they were alone.

"Sure, son, what is it?" Roy knew his son well enough to know that whatever he had to say would have importance.

"I ... don't think my eyes were playing tricks on me," Josh struggled to find the right words. "I'm ... pretty sure ... no, I'm positive. I saw somebody up on the mountain, just when the slide started!"

"Are you absolutely sure?" Roy was stunned by the news.

"As sure as I can be, Dad," Josh nodded firmly. "A lot was happening at once, but I just know I caught a glimpse of somebody up there."

Roy Douglas rubbed his chin for a long time.

"Anybody you would recognize?" he finally asked.

"No, whoever it was was just too far away," Josh shook his head.

"Well," Roy spoke slowly, "I guess there are several possible explanations.

"Could be just a coincidence," he surmised, "or it could have been some hiker who accidentally started the slide or...," he paused thoughtfully.

"Or it could have been deliberate," he concluded.

They walked on a little further, arrived at the liner and climbed up into the cab.

Before starting the truck, Roy stared for a long time out the windshield into the black mountain night.

"We better keep this to ourselves for a while," he told Josh. "If this slide was deliberate, it could be that some maniac gets his jollies out of trying to bury passing motorists.

"Or," he paused ominously, "it could be that the slide was meant for us!"

Chapter Eight

In spite of the near-tragedy and resulting delay from the Rogers Pass incident, the Cloverdale Rodeo got off to a good start.

The horses and bulls had weathered the long trip well and had so far been outstanding. Numerous cowboys had suffered spectacular, and sometimes painful, spills before the sound of the eight-second klaxon.

Others had been able to ride the feisty D Lazy D animals and the results for some had been exceptional. Several scores in the eighties had been registered during the rodeo's first four performances.

Through it all the younger members of the

Douglas Rodeo entourage had been busy. C. J., who just a year earlier had received his own baptism into the sport, appointed himself official tour guide and rodeo interpreter for the newest "rookie" on the Douglas team.

During each performance he and Rudolph perched themselves in strategic vantage points and C. J. proceeded to fill the younger boy's ears with non-stop rodeo facts, statistics and trivia.

"Cloverdale is one of Canada's most important rodeos," he explained to Rudolph the first day. "There are five rodeos that make up a special Pro Rodeo Series. Out of the series the top five cowboys in each event qualify for the fifty thousand dollar rideoff on the final Sunday of the Calgary Stampede."

"You mean a cowboy can win fifty thousand dollars in one day?" Rudolph exclaimed.

"I mean a cowboy can win fifty thousand dollars in eight seconds," C. J. stated dramatically, obviously enjoying his role as rodeo expert.

Rudolph, for his part, was a willing but sometimes frustrating pupil.

Occasionally his questions would have aggravated even the most patient of teachers. There were times when C. J. was hard-pressed to remain civil when the European visitor's queries seemed utterly pointless.

"Did you say that little rope with which the calf-roper ties the calf's legs is called a piggin' string?" Rudolph asked at one point.

"That's right!" C. J. beamed his pleasure at his prize pupil's ability to learn. His joy quickly turned to despair as Rudolph went on.

"But it seems to me it ought to be called a calfin' string. There isn't a pig in sight," was his resolute conclusion.

Later, during the Saddle Bronc Riding event, a cowboy was awarded a re-ride when the horse he drew simply didn't buck. Re-rides are a stock contractor's nightmare and C. J. felt a little depressed at the poor performance by one of the Douglas mares.

Rudolph was ecstatic. "I'll bet he'll receive a wonderful score for that one, right C. J.?" he said enthusiastically.

"Are you kidding?" C. J. moaned. "The horse didn't buck or jump. I told you half the score is for the cowboy and half for the horse. He'll have to ride again on a different horse. Horses are like people. They can have bad days too." C. J.'s voice indicated his disappointment.

"But that's just it!" Rudolph was still excited. "He tamed that horse, that cowboy did. Surely, that should be worth one hundred and fifty points."

C. J. held his head in disbelief, "The maximum is one hundred points, I told you. Look, if the horse doesn't buck ... aw, forget it. You want some ice cream or somethin'?"

"You bet, pardner," Rudolph proudly practised some of his newly learned rodeo jargon as C. J. gritted his teeth.

The final straw came after the third performance when everyone was gathered in the Douglas motorhome over dinner.

"I have a question, C. J.," Rudolph announced between bites of chicken and dumplings.

C. J. eyed him suspiciously before replying, "Okay, shoot!"

"Well, I'm a bit puzzled," Rudolph began. "Why is it that when the Barrel Racing began you told me it was a really boring event, and yet when Cindy made her run today you got so excited you fell off the fence?"

Rudolph looked at C. J. in wide-eyed innocence; around the table there were several suppressed snickers.

A deep pink color rose in C. J.'s cheeks as he glared at the speaker. He tried twice to answer the charge, but words failed him.

He glanced shyly at Cindy across the table but she was concentrating hard on her plate, a deep blush having invaded her cheeks too. Everyone at the ranch knew about the romance between the two teen-age sweethearts and they thoroughly enjoyed every opportunity to tease C. J. about it.

Rudolph's seemingly innocent question made him an instant ally of Jenny, the leading participant in the teasing department.

"Atta boy, Rudolph," she slapped him on the back. "You're gonna fit in just fine around here. But, what's this about Barrel Racing being boring?" She stared at C. J. in mock anger.

"Yes, what a terrible thing to say, C. J.," Cindy chipped in, further adding to the boy's discomfort.

"I ... didn't mean ... uh ... that is ... well, what I mean is ... "

The rest of his reply was drowned out by laughter. Even C. J. had to admit that Rudolph had put one over on him that time.

The last day of the Cloverdale Rodeo was an important one for everyone involved with the Douglas Rodeo Company.

Because it was a Series Rodeo, the last performance was actually a finals. The ten best cowboys from the first four performances in each of the major events, Bareback and Saddle Bronc Riding, Calf Roping, Steer Wrestling and Bull Riding would be back to contest the finals. Their cumulative scores or times for the two rides or runs would determine the rodeo's champions.

The five Series rodeos were televised nationally as well, so everyone wanted to put his best foot forward. Roy Douglas and pickup men Len Tucker and Ben Bradley took extra pains to look good before the cameras.

To add to the excitement, Jenny, Josh and C. J. were all scheduled to compete during the final performance.

Cindy had already competed as Rudolph had so adeptly pointed out during the dinner conversation the previous day. Unfortunately, she had knocked down a barrel, giving her a five-second penalty and taking her out of the money.

The sun quickly warmed the rodeo grounds as the large crowd filed in and took up their places in the grandstand and bleachers that flanked the arena.

As the minutes ticked down to rodeo time, nervous cowboys paced back and forth behind the chutes or warmed up their horses in the arena.

Roy and his hands cut out the stock that had been drawn for that day into holding pens. The bareback horses, first on the program, were loaded in the bucking chutes.

Like the cowboys, they seemed to be able to sense the tension in the air and stamped and snorted with impatience.

Jenny was at the motorhome in the infield behind the arena. She was grooming Sugar in preparation for her run. Neither the Barrel Racing nor the Boys' Steer Riding were part of the Series, so there was no finals. Each contestant competed only once. For Jenny, Josh and C. J., today was their one chance and each wanted desperately to succeed.

The two steer riders were behind the chutes copying every move of their grown-up cowboy heroes. They did the same warm-up exercises and prepared their ropes the same way. Josh had even taken to wearing suspenders when competing because a couple of his favorite bull riders did so.

The rodeo began with the spectacular grand entry, the traditional parading of the flags and ride past of the contestants. The national anthem was sung and the rodeo was underway.

Josh, C. J. and Rudolph stayed behind the chutes

as the two young cowboys made their final pre-parations. Though concentrating on their own activity, all three heads turned whenever the roar of the crowd announced a great ride or spectacular fall.

In the background the excited voice of announcer Hank Parker kept the crowd informed of the identity of the contestants, the stock each had drawn and the score that each rider achieved.

At the same time Rudolph kept up a steady stream of conversation in the form of questions directed at C.J. and Josh.

His excitement about their impending rides was as great as, or perhaps greater than, that of his two friends.

"What's that?"

"It's resin, we put it on the ropes."

"What for?"

"It's to help us grip the rope better."

"Do the steers bite?"

"No Rudolph, they don't bite."

"Are you frightened?"

"Not really, just sort of nervous."

"Is it time yet?"

"Not yet, Rudolph. There are two more events until it's our turn."

And so it went. Finally, it was time. Roy Douglas called over the chutes, "Okay steer riders, your stock is in the chutes; let's get ready."

As they started for the chutes, C. J. suddenly pushed Josh gently with his elbow. "Look who's here," he whispered.

Off to their right was the sneering profile of Miles Shivers, his unmistakable strut carrying him towards the chutes. He hadn't spotted Josh and C. J. yet.

Josh purposely changed directions so as to intercept his long-time adversary. He stopped directly in front of Miles, who stood a couple of inches taller and outweighed Josh by probably twenty-five pounds.

"What do you want, Douglas?" Miles Shivers snarled at Josh.

"Just wondered why you and your brother didn't drop in when you were by our place last week." Josh's voice contained no trace of its usual warmth.

For an instant Miles Shivers' eyes opened wide in surprise but he recovered quickly.

"What are you yappin' about now, Douglas? We wouldn't be caught dead around that dump you call a ranch."

Josh took a step towards the bigger boy. "That's not the way I hear it, Shivers. I hear you were..."

"Come on, Josh," C. J. grabbed his arm. "Our steers are in. We gotta go."

"I see you've got your wimp cousin with you again, Douglas." Miles looked disdainfully at C. J. "Sure hope you don't fall down and hurt yourself ... Clayton."

Miles put special emphasis on the last word as if to

show his contempt for C. J. Now it was Josh's turn to step between his cousin and their sworn enemy.

"By the way, Shivers," Josh said over his shoulder as he firmly guided C. J. towards the chutes, "I haven't seen your brother around lately. In fact, he didn't even enter the rodeo. I hope it's not because the Douglas bulls are too tough for him."

"Don't worry Douglas," Miles Shivers gestured with his fist, "when the time comes, you'll see all of my brother you want to and then some."

Both Josh and C. J. wondered what Miles' threat meant but they didn't have time to trade further verbal jibes.

Josh was to ride first so he and C. J. sprinted to chute number three where a brown-and-white Hereford steer was waiting.

Both pickup men weren't required in the arena during the steer riding, so Len Tucker was waiting at the chute to help the boys get ready.

Seventy-two points was the leading score heading into the final day. Both boys wanted to win badly, Josh to move further out in front of the Canadian standings and C. J. to climb into the top six in the standings. Only the top six steer riders for the year would be eligible for the Canadian Finals Rodeo at season's end.

Josh dropped his bull rope down alongside the steer. With Len's help he hooked the tail of the rope and brought it up and around the other side. Then he sat down on the back of the steer and as C. J. held one end in the air, he warmed the well-resined rope. Len stood at the head of the steer to quiet it if it became jumpy in the chutes.

Behind Josh in chute one, the first steer rider had nodded and was in the arena. Bullfighter Tub Willoughby in his outlandish costume was running alongside as the steer bucked.

Just before the klaxon sounded, the unfortunate rider was dumped unceremoniously to the ground.

Quickly Tub placed himself between the steer and the "displaced," disappointed cowboy. Tub removed his hat and to the crowd's delight fanned the seat of the steer rider's pants – presumably to cool it off.

As the second steer rider made his ride, Josh took his hand hold and with C. J.'s help took the free end of the rope into his palms again. He was ready. With all his concentration now on the steer, Josh heard only vaguely the voice of Hank Parker announcing the score for the last contestant as 63 points.

"Okay, Josh, ride like you can now," C. J. encouraged him.

"Use your feet," Len offered the advice that every steer rider receives prior to his ride.

Rudolph had climbed up on the back of the chute to stand next to C. J. "Cowboy up, Josh," he called in his high-pitched voice.

C. J. looked at him. "Cowboy up? Where did you learn that?"

"I heard somebody say that to the last rider," Rudolph shrugged and grinned. "I thought it sounded rather appropriate."

Outside the chute, Roy Douglas had ridden up and now looked over the chute gate. "Okay, Josh, the arena's clear; let's go," he said in a businesslike voice.

Over the arena sound system, Josh heard Hank Parker's, "Out of chute number three comes the cowboy who is leading the Canadian Steer Riding standings ... Josh Douglas."

Josh slid forward on his rope and nodded. The gate swung open and the steer catapulted into action. It started with a high jump, then kicked out its hind legs and landed hard on its front. It was what the cowboys called a trashy steer, throwing a lot of ducks and dives at its rider. Josh stuck like glue and was never really in any danger of being bucked off. As the klaxon sounded, he threw his right leg up and rolled off to the left of the steer, landing squarely at the feet of Tub Willoughby. The genial clown offered the "high five" to signal his approval for the ride.

Josh reached high and smacked his hand against Tub's. Then he turned and ran back to the chutes as quickly as his chaps would allow in order to help C. J. who was already getting ready in chute five.

As Josh climbed up the chute and over to the back, Hank Parker told the crowd "70 points for Josh Douglas, good for second place so far."

C. J. cast Josh a quick congratulatory smile as behind them the rider from chute number four made a short-lived journey into the arena.

"Okay, C. J., this steer will be just what you want," said Josh, "I've seen him before and he should come around to the right."

It was a big Charolais steer and was acting up a little in the chute. "Get out on 'im quick; I won't be able to hold 'im long," Len Tucker urged from in front of the steer where he had a powerful arm wrapped around the animal's neck.

C. J. was ready and nodded quickly. In the arena, the steer was just as Josh had predicted. It didn't buck high or hard but the spin to the right made it difficult to ride.

C. J. worked desperately at trying to stay in the middle of the steer's back as the sheer force of the spin forced him more and more to the left.

At last the steer got him tipped over to the left side and C. J. was thrown off landing hard on his shoulder just as the klaxon blared.

The fall shook him up but he wasn't hurt. He jumped up quickly to look to the judges who would indicate whether he had still been aboard the steer at the eight-second signal. They were nodding!

"69 points," called Hank Parker, "Good for third place and a share of the prize money for the kid from Toronto."

Josh pumped C. J.'s hand up and down. He was as excited as his cousin was with the solid result.

Both boys stayed in the arena to get a close-up view of Miles Shivers' ride. While they fervently hoped he would be unsuccessful, they were aware that he was one of the better steer riders and could well wind up winning the rodeo.

The gate to chute number six opened and a stocky reddish-brown steer came into the arena running hard with Miles Shivers, teeth gritted, jabbing his heels furiously into the animal's sides.

Suddenly, without warning, the steer went straight up into the air and with a twisting motion came down facing the opposite direction. As quickly as it had begun, Miles' ride was over as he was crashed down into the arena dirt.

The event was over with Josh placing second and C. J. third, his best result ever.

C. J. had one piece of unfinished business to attend to. As Miles Shivers made his way back to the chutes, kicking dirt and cursing all the way, C. J. called out in a syrupy sweet voice, "I'm sure sorry you fell off that wimp steer there, Miles. Hope you didn't hurt yourself."

Hatred blazed in the eyes of Miles Shivers as he glared at C. J. and Josh. He started toward them, then apparently thought better of it and headed off in the opposite direction.

"Hey, let's see what Rudolph thought of our performance," Josh nudged C. J. in the ribs and together they climbed back over the chutes to where they'd left Canada's newest and most excitable rodeo fan. Dropping in behind the chutes, their bantering and kibitzing quickly ended to be replaced by concern and then outright alarm.

Rudolph was gone!

Chapter Nine

A twinge of panic crept over the two boys causing each to shiver. Maybe Rudolph had just gone for a snack or to the bathroom. Still, a lot of strange things had been happening....

Josh looked around quickly.

He spotted Len Tuck- er who was getting ready to mount his horse and head back into the arena.

"Have you seen Rudolph?" Josh asked him.

"He was here just a few minutes ago," Len replied, throwing his leg up over the saddle. "Sorry I can't help you look right now. Gotta go."

Josh and C. J. grabbed a couple of passing cow-boys. "Did you guys see a little kid around here . . . dressed kind of funny . . . wearing short pants?" C. J. inquired.

"Nope, not me," said the first. "Sorry."

"Yeah ... I did, come to think of it," the second answered slowly, pausing to spit tobacco juice on the ground. "He lit out that way a coupla minutes ago ... travellin' fast as I recall."

"Thanks!" chorused the cousins as they hurried off in the direction the cowboy had indicated.

They checked first at the concession stand and found no sign of Rudolph. Next they checked the bathroom area. He wasn't there either.

They split up and circled the infield, meeting a few minutes later back behind the chutes.

"Any ... sign of him?" Josh gasped for air as he questioned C. J.

"Not a trace," puffed C. J., equally out of breath. "What'll we do? I'm getting worried."

"Me too! C'mon, let's try over by the motorhome," Josh suggested. This time they ran off at top speed.

They had just arrived at the motorhome when Rudolph came from around the other side running as hard as his short legs could carry him.

His face was a picture of terror. When he saw Josh and C. J., he altered his course so as to end up right between them, where he fell in an exhausted heap.

"Help me!" he sputtered.

"What's the matter?" Josh asked as he and C. J. assisted the panic-stricken boy to his feet. Before Rudolph could reply, a second figure hurried from between some vehicles and came around the side of the motorhome.

He was a stranger to Josh and C. J.; it was obvious

that he had been chasing Rudolph. The boy cowered behind Josh.

The man was large, had a reddish complexion and eyes that were narrow slits. He never took them off Rudolph.

The stranger looked to be about ten years older than Roy Douglas. He was wearing a trench coat and hat, both of which seemed oddly out of place on such a hot day. He attempted to smile at the three boys, but the look made him appear even more evil than he already did.

"Who are you?" C. J. demanded.

"Get out of my way boys," the man replied in a heavily accented voice. "You are interfering where you do not belong. The boy is to be with me."

He took a step forward. Both C. J. and Josh placed themselves in such a way as to block the stranger's path to Rudolph.

"Do not try my patience, young gentlemen," the man threatened. "I will deal with you if I am forced to."

Josh's voice had the determined Douglas edge to it when he said, "Mister, I don't know who you are, but you're going to have to create a whole lot of commotion to get him away from us and I've got a hunch you don't want that."

Behind them a pickup truck slammed to a halt and a second man raced up to the first, then stopped in total surprise when he saw Josh and C. J.

It was Lefty Shivers!

"Well, well," C. J. greeted him cheerfully, "we were wondering where you had got to. Why, we were asking your brother whatever had become of you just today, weren't we Josh?"

"I figured if something rotten was goin' on, you'd have to be in on it somewhere Shivers!" Josh spat the words.

"Let's grab the kid," Lefty urged the older man. "I can handle these two punks."

He started forward. Josh and C. J. braced themselves for a fight they knew they could only lose.

Their only hope was for help to arrive; not a very likely possibility with the rodeo still going on.

But help did arrive. As Lefty moved towards the three boys, suddenly from between vehicles, with a wild shriek, came Jenny thundering at them on Sugar.

Lefty halted in surprise but before he could react, Jenny had ridden straight into him, knocking the surprised cowboy back several feet and landing him flat on his back.

As the first man tried to flee, Jenny wheeled her mount and charged again. She just missed the huge stranger, who was barely able to take shelter in the doorway of the motorhome.

Now Lefty, a little stunned and bleeding from the nose, staggered to his feet. Jenny saw him, turned and charged again. Lefty caught sight of her and at the last second dived to safety under the motorhome.

In spite of the danger they had found themselves in, the boys were nearly doubled over with laughter. "I think the cavalry has arrived," C. J. hooted.

"Let's go," said Josh, as he grabbed Rudolph and they started quickly back toward the infield.

"Atta girl, Jenny!" C. J. shouted over his shoulder as he joined Josh and Rudolph. Quickly the three of them made their getaway.

Back at the motorhome, the man in the dark trench coat tried a couple of times to escape to the safety of the pickup truck in which Lefty had arrived. Each time, however, he was forced to scamper back to the motorhome as Jenny thundered by on Sugar missing him by just centimetres.

Looking back, Jenny could see that the three boys were almost back to the infield. She pulled her horse to a halt and patted her on the neck.

"Good girl," she said loudly. "That should be a good enough warm-up for the Barrel Racing."

With that she turned and, with her red hair bobbing nonchalantly up and down, trotted primly away on Sugar.

As soon as they were safely back in the infield, Josh grabbed Rudolph's arm.

"Who was that creep anyway?"

"I... I don't... know," Rudolph stammered.

"He sure seemed to know you," C. J. said.

"I ... I've never seen him before." Rudolph avoided looking at either of them as he spoke.

"Something awfully funny is goin' on around here," said Josh, staring hard at Rudolph. "First, the Shivers boys are hangin' around our place and you're divin' for cover when airplanes fly over.

"Then there's a rock slide that nearly kills you and Len. And now it looks like Lefty Shivers is tied up with some character with a foreign accent, and they're both after you but you don't know why or who the guy is. I think we better plan on sitting down and having a long talk with Dad as soon as the rodeo's over," Josh said firmly.

"And until then, you better plan to stick to us like glue," C. J. added, taking the smaller boy's other arm.

"Let's go watch the rest of the rodeo," Josh suggested and the three of them took up a place on the fence next to the bucking chutes.

The barrel racing was already underway. Two girls had already made their runs and it was Jenny's turn.

She came into the arena through a gate right next to where the three boys were sitting. The look on her face gave no indication of what had happened just moments earlier. She was looking out at the triangular pattern of the barrels in the infield.

"Make a run, Jenny," C. J. encouraged.

"C'mon sis, be rapid," Josh called to his twin.

For once, Rudolph showed no sign of excitement at all. He sat glumly with his chin on his hands.

His small body was almost unseen, so tightly Josh and C. J. had him squeezed between them.

Jenny made one small circle on Sugar, then urged the mare into action, sprinting full out to the first barrel.

She would make a turn to the right around the first barrel, then two turns to the left around the remaining barrels, before running full-out for home. It was a quick event, over usually in around fifteen seconds. There was little or no margin for error as the Barrel Racing was often decided by tenths of a second.

Unlike the other events, which paid anywhere from four to eight places, the Barrel Racing paid ten. While it was a little easier to place, the amount of money won dropped off quickly in the lower placings.

To make matters doubly difficult for Jenny was the fact that she was racing against the cream of

Canada's Barrel Racers as well as many of the top girls from the United States.

Although Jenny didn't have the experience of many of her competitors, she was as capable a horse-woman as anyone there. In addition she was a fiercely determined competitor, an important trait in this pull-out-all-the-stops event.

As they reached the first barrel, Jenny slid her right hand up the rein to help Sugar around the barrel. Her left hand was gripped fast to the saddle horn, to help her absorb the horse's power as it pulled hard away from the barrel.

Sugar formed a perfect arc around the first barrel. The game little mare came away in perfect position to race to the second.

At the second barrel Jenny was forced to switch hands as the process was now reversed; she and Sugar made the first of their two left-hand turns.

As the pair glided fluidly around the second barrel, Josh and C. J. edged forward on the top rail of the fence. Jenny was having a great run!

"Come on, Jen!" Josh shouted excitedly.

"What does she have to beat?" C. J. asked Josh, neither of them letting his eyes leave Jenny for even an instant.

"14.98 seconds," Josh told him. "But the third barrel is where she usually has her trouble."

They leaned forward still further. Rudolph, in spite of his dreading of what would take place after the rodeo, could contain himself no longer.

He jumped up on the top rail. "Go, Jenny, go!" he screamed.

The crowd, sensing that Jenny's run was good, was also roaring encouragement to the young contestant.

Jenny and Sugar arrived at the third barrel in full stride.

"She's going too fast to turn it." Josh clenched his fists as Jenny prepared to turn.

Sugar dug in her hind quarters, and swung around hard. As she did, her shoulder gave the barrel a hard rap.

It teetered uncertainly on edge as Jenny and Sugar completed the turn and headed for home.

For a split second, the crowd was silent. It was as if ten thousand people had held their breaths all at once. Speeding for home, Jenny glanced back. The barrel was still tottering; then it lurched back upright. An immense cheer went up from the crowd.

Jenny knew from the cheer that the barrel couldn't have fallen. She put her head down low over Sugar's neck and hissed in the quarter horse's ear to ask for speed. They blazed across the finish line! Again the arena fell silent as everyone waited for Hank Parker, who had himself been pretty excited during Jenny's run, to announce her time.

"Ladies and gentlemen, we have a new leader! Jenny Douglas with a time of 14.96 takes the lead by two-hundredths of a second."

C. J., Josh and Rudolph slumped back to their

seats, drained by the tension of Jenny's performance.

"I'll tell you one thing," C. J. heaved a huge sigh, "I don't think I can stand much more excitement today."

Beside him Rudolph chuckled softly, then said, "Well, my Canadian friends, I'm afraid you're in for a little more before this day's over."

Chapter Ten

Roy Douglas tossed another log on the bonfire. The Douglas family, the rodeo hands and guests Cindy and Rudolph were gathered in a loose circle around the fire.

Everyone in the family loved a campfire and tonight's was a special one. Roy had declared a celebration in honor of two happy events. First the Cloverdale Rodeo had been a large success. The committee that had worked so hard to put the rodeo together had been delighted with the stock and the work of everyone from the Douglas Rodeo Company. That was reason enough for jubilation.

But more important to the members of the close-knit Douglas family was the first professional Barrel Racing win for Jenny.

In honor of the event, Laura Douglas had cooked Jenny's favorite meal, fried chicken. Josh, C. J. and Cindy had contributed to the event by baking a cake. Rudolph and Len Tucker, soul mates since their ordeal beneath the rock slide, teamed up to ice the cake.

Their attempts at being artistic were, in Laura Douglas' words "interesting," in Jenny's "gross."

Ben Bradley had carved several marshmallow sticks and now the family was toasting marshmallows and relaxing in the double glow of the fire and success.

Roy topped up his coffee, leaned back in his lawn chair and said, "All right boys, I'm ready to hear your story."

He had steadfastly refused to hear what C. J. and Josh had had to say earlier. He hadn't wanted anything to take away from Jenny's moment of glory.

Now, after three pieces of chicken and two generous hunks of cake, he was ready to listen.

And listen he did, first to the boys recounting of what happened after they discovered that Rudolph had disappeared. Then he heard Jenny's rather colorful retelling of her horseback encounter with the big foreign man and Lefty Shivers.

"Sugar and me, we put the run on 'em," she concluded her story triumphantly.

Roy stared up at the night sky for a long time. Finally, after several swallows of coffee, he turned to Rudolph and said gently, "Well son, I guess it's about time you told us the truth, wouldn't you say?"

Rudolph poked his marshmallow stick at the fire. "Yes Sir, I believe you're right," he answered.

No one pushed or prodded him. Most went on cooking their marshmallows as if he were relating a fishing story to the group.

"First of all," he began slowly, "I'm not really from Austria. I live in a little principality that borders on Austria and Switzerland. It's called Mendenstein. You may not have even heard of it. It's very small, only about two hundred and fifty kilometres from one end to the other.

"We have a system of government very similar to what exists in Switzerland, with a governing council in charge of making many of the decisions.

"There is one very important difference, however, in our system. In Mendenstein we have a Royal Family. As you are probably aware, there are very few remaining monarchies in Europe or, for that matter, in the world. Ours is a little different than your British monarchy in that our reigning King has more power in the government, though his is not the sole or even the greatest power.

"For the past thirteen years the man on the throne of Mendenstein has been Prince Ludwig IV."

Rudolph paused and stared at the end of the marshmallow stick, now glowing red. Then he looked around at the faces of the people who had been listening intently as he spoke.

"I am his son," he said in a voice that could barely be heard in the still night.

"You mean ... you're the Prince's son?" C. J. stammered incredulously.

"But that makes you... a...," Jenny couldn't make herself say the word.

"Prince, too," Josh breathed.

Rudolph reached inside his back pocket and pulled out a beat-up hunk of folded paper. He passed it to Roy Douglas who hadn't spoken since Rudolph had begun to relate his story.

As Roy unfolded the paper, the others could see it was a newspaper clipping. He leaned closer to the fire and scanned the yellowed clipping.

After reading for a few seconds, he looked over at Rudolph whose attention was once again on the fire.

Roy looked back to the clipping and began to read. "Winnipeg Free Press, May 3rd," he began. "Today marked the beginning of a royal visit to our city. His Highness Prince Ludwig IV of the Principality of Mendenstein, accompanied by the eleven-year-old Crown Prince Rolf, will spend the next day and a half in Winnipeg before travelling to Alberta for a Rocky Mountain fishing and hiking holiday.

"The royal pair are in Canada to promote cultural ties between the two long-time international allies. They will be visiting City Hall, two art galleries and a museum before attending the Royal Winnipeg Ballet's performance of William Tell this evening."

Roy looked up. "There's a picture of the Prince and the Crown Prince," he added. "There's no question... it seems like our friend Rudolph is actually Prince Rolf of Mendenstein."

No one knew quite what to say or do. Len Tucker solemnly removed his hat. Ben Bradley pulled his tobacco plug from his mouth and threw it to the ground. Josh whistled and Jenny sighed a huge "Wow!"

"My story, of course, isn't nearly complete," Rudolph said calmly. "You'll want to know why I deceived you and why a number of things have happened since I arrived."

He tossed his stick into the fire. "The newspaper article is accurate," he continued. "My father and I *did* go to Banff, and I told you the truth about his having to leave.

"Of course, he didn't go to Vienna but home to Mendenstein. The reason was some crisis of government which I don't really understand. However, the truth is that I wasn't left here alone, as I told you.

"The man we encountered today is Baron Steg ... a senior member of my father's governing council. He holds the position of Minister of Foreign Relations. I was left in his care when my father left for home.

"I have suspected for a long time that Baron Steg did not have our people's best interests at heart. I thought that he was trying to gain more power for himself. A couple of days after my father left, I overheard a conversation between Baron Steg and two of the men in our delegation that frightened me terribly.

"I heard him tell the others that under no circumstance was I to see Mendenstein ever again, alive. I ran away. All I took was what you have seen. The money was my own that my father had left with me to buy presents for my mother.

"I had no idea where to go. I hid in the back of a pickup truck that was leaving Banff. I didn't know where it was going and I almost froze in the back of that truck.

"I jumped out at a gas station and began walking, and the first person I saw was Mr. Levy. He very kindly allowed me to stay with him until he delivered me to your ranch."

No one had moved a muscle during the time this strange tale was being told.

"Did you try to contact your father ... the Prince?" Laura Douglas asked.

"Yes, I did," came the reply, "but I'm sure you can appreciate that it's extremely difficult, even for me, to simply place a call to the ruler of my country. I reached his personal secretary, Herr Meyerling, twice. Each time he refused to connect me with my father. He gave excuses that he was in high-level conferences and could not be disturbed.

"Then he would ask me many questions. I believe he was trying to find out where I was so that he could let Baron Steg know. I am convinced that they are working together."

"For what?" Roy asked pointedly. "What would this Baron Steg gain from having you ... uh ... removed?"

"It's quite simple," the Prince replied. "I am the last in my line. We have no other family. If I were eliminated and something were to happen to my father, the power in my country would fall directly to the Governing Council.

"Baron Steg and Herr Meyerling are two of the most powerful men in the Council. They could have the monarchy abolished and themselves declared President and Prime Minister.

"It would happen very quickly, I can assure you."

"Why didn't you go to the R.C.M.P. with your suspicions?" Roy asked.

"Or someone else in your delegation," Ben Bradley added. "There must have been someone you could trust."

"This is an incident of astounding importance to my country," the Prince answered. "It could also be, I regret, a matter of considerable humiliation that this kind of intrigue is going on in our government, particularly if it were to become public.

"As for the rest of our delegation," he turned to Ben, "I was no longer sure of anyone I could trust. If I had confided in someone what I knew and guessed wrong about that person..." He left out the rest of the frightening thought.

"I was convinced I had one course of action open to me," the Prince continued. "I had to try to hide from them until I could get to Toronto. You see, my father is coming back at the end of July and we will be flying home together." His voice dropped to barely more than a whisper, " If I can just make it until then ... I'd have a chance if you would help me."

It wasn't a plea; it was a simple statement of fact.

"By the way," the Prince added. "That is why I stalled for time and missed the television interview after the rockslide. Obviously, it was important that I avoid appearing on national television where I could have been seen by Baron Steg or his men."

All eyes around the campfire moved from the boy from Mendenstein to Roy Douglas. He was obviously wrestling with the problem.

"Well," he spoke even more slowly than usual, "let's reflect on this a minute. First of all, there's no doubt about it, this young man hasn't been truthful with us up to now.

"So we've got to decide, first, *if* he's being truthful now and second, *if* he is telling the truth, what do we do with a Prince on the run?"

"I believe him Dad," Jenny said quietly.

"Me too," echoed Josh.

"So do I," C. J. was next.

Ben, Cindy and Len were all nodding their heads in agreement.

Laura Douglas crossed to where the strangest visitor they had ever had was sitting. She reached down and took his hand. "I believe him too, Roy."

Roy Douglas loved his children and cherished his friends, but he adored his wife. If she trusted this young man, there was no longer any question in his mind. "Well, I'm glad you all feel that way, because I believe him too," he grinned at the gathering around the fire that was beginning to die out.

"It looks like you're a part of the family, son," he told the smiling Prince. "We'll do everything we can to look after you."

Len Tucker spoke up, "I'm guessing they won't bother us out at the ranch as long as we're careful. I figure Baron Steg and his bunch will probably make their move in a big place, like at the Calgary Stampede or maybe Toronto.

"I think those are the places we're really going to have to be on our guard."

"Sounds reasonable to me, Len," Roy concurred. "But that doesn't mean you can head off for a ride over the hills by yourself," he told the Prince.

"From now on," he went on, "you will have to have at least one of us with you everywhere you go. I hope you don't mind ... uh ... say, what do we call you anyway?"

"I'll bet it's Your Highness, Dad." Jenny, as always, was sure of herself.

"I'd really prefer Rolf," the Prince responded. "It would be rather nice to hear my name for a change."

"Yeah, to tell you the truth I wasn't that crazy about the name Rudolph," Jenny agreed. Suddenly, the red-haired teen screamed in anguish.

"What's wrong?" asked Laura Douglas. "Did you burn yourself?"

"No," Jenny answered, wringing her hands.

"I just realized that I was calling the future ruler of Mendenstein 'Sawbones'." She shook her head miserably. "Can you ever forgive me, Your Highness?"

Rolf led the laughter that followed by saying, "Jenny, after your performance with Baron Steg today, I can forgive you for anything."

"Hey, I just thought of something" C. J. interjected. "How did the Shivers boys get into this?"

"Good question," Roy Douglas replied. "No doubt they've been recruited by Baron Steg because they're his kind of guys.

"We'll have to be on our toes," he warned... "the next two months are going to be interesting, to say the least."

A long, narrow log in the fire crackled loudly as the flames burned through.

Chapter Eleven

C. J. lay wide awake. He had been in that state for at least an hour.

The first day of the Calgary Stampede brought with it a combination of nervousness and excitement that was making sleep impossible.

After a few more minutes of squirming, he gave up trying to sleep and sat up, craning his neck to see out the window of the motorhome. The pre-dawn semi-darkness was just beginning to disappear. No one else seemed to be having any difficulty as the sounds of deep sleep filled the still motorhome. Next to C. J., Rolf lay on his side, his boyish countenance relaxed in slumber, giving no hint of the turmoil that seemed to swirl around the Prince at his every move.

C. J. softly slid back the covers and climbed carefully out of the bed. The clock on the counter indicated that more than half an hour would pass before six a.m.

Quickly and quietly dressing, C. J. stepped out of the motorhome into the cool morning air. A gentle west wind whispered through the grass of the infield.

To his right the enormous Stampede grandstand rose like a modern-day pyramid out of the haze-bound skyscrapers in the background. Around him, the infield of the Stampede grounds had yet to come alive. What in a few short hours would be a marketplace of activity, was for the moment a silent campground, the stillness broken only now and then by the passing of a loud vehicle on Macleod Trail, the artery that bordered the western edge of the grounds.

C. J. could still see in his mind's eye that grandstand one year before, each afternoon filled to the brim with cheering rodeo fans, each evening with the thousands who thrilled to the spectacular Stampede chuckwagon races and grandstand show.

He had never seen that grandstand or this infield the way he was seeing it now. Strangely, the scene around him was somehow as thrilling, though in a very different way, as that magnificent spectacle that had awed him so much one year before.

He slowly zig-zagged his way through the campers. Eventually, he came out into the rodeo infield itself. His heart began to race as he drifted across it towards the chutes.

Once he kicked a little dirt, then quickly smoothed over the spot, almost ashamed at having disturbed the serenity of the moment. Reaching the chutes, he climbed up the front of Chute Number Seven and, turning around, sat on the rail, surveying the arena, stage and grandstand across from him.

The Calgary Stampede! The words were enough to send shudders of excitement through even the most hardened cowboy. C. J. heaved a long, contented sigh, leaned his elbows easily on his knees, and in a state of happiness he would have had difficulty describing, began recapping in his mind the events of the last several weeks.

At the D Lazy D, the level of activity had intensified as the ten days of the Stampede had drawn nearer.

Roy Douglas and the Douglas rodeo hands had worked long hours readying the stock and equipment for "The Greatest Outdoor Show on Earth."

C. J., Josh, Jenny and Cindy had used every available moment to practise. As the days were at their longest through the last weeks of June, there had been plenty of opportunity to hone steer riding skills and work barrel racing horses.

Within minutes of the school bus dropping them off at the driveway in front of the Douglas ranch house, the four young competitors and Rolf, their trainer and head cheerleader, were racing for the practice pens.

June had brought with it more rodeos and had taken them to places like Lea Park, Coronation, Wainwright and one long haul all the way to Brandon, Manitoba.

Len Tucker's prediction had held true. No further incidents had taken place; in fact, there had been absolutely no sign of Baron Steg or either of the Shivers boys since the Cloverdale episode.

Nevertheless, Roy Douglas had insisted that all of them keep up their guard. Rolf had joined Josh, Jenny and C. J. in attending the local school and through the entire month of June, a member of the Douglas family or one of the hands followed the bus into High River each morning.

When school was dismissed for the day, the same precaution had been taken. In each case, the following vehicle had stayed well back from the bus in order not to arouse suspicion from any of Baron Steg's hoodlums who might have been observing the movements of the bus and its passengers.

On the front seat of the pickup truck had been a loaded rifle. It was the only time in his life Roy Douglas had ever permitted a weapon to be carried for any purpose besides hunting.

As Rolf was just a visitor at school — he had completed his school term before coming to Canada — he had been permitted to sit in on the classes of Josh, Jenny and C. J. Laura Douglas had made the arrangement to ensure that Rolf was never alone, even in the relative safety of the school.

Much to the chagrin of his three hosts, Rolf had quickly established himself as one of the brightest pupils in the class. He was especially gifted in the areas of English, mathematics, science and European history. Jenny, in particular, had been miffed at having been displaced as the top student in the class. Still her complaining had been of the good-natured variety, thrilled as she was to have a royal visitor staying at the ranch.

It was hard to know which was most exciting to her – knowing that Rolf was a Prince, or keeping that knowledge a secret from her school friends.

Under strict orders from Roy Douglas, not even the teachers had been permitted to know the real story. Rolf had been sketchily introduced as a distant Douglas relative from Europe.

For his own part, Rolf had been very good at not giving out any but the barest information about himself. Whenever the questions had become too intense, he had resorted to a convenient "*kann ich nicht verstehen*" which Jenny or C. J. had been only to happy to translate as "I don't understand."

While the June rodeo schedule had been routine from the standpoint of intrigue, there had been plenty of excitement nevertheless.

At Lea Park, Jenny and Josh had scored a rare brother-sister double, both of them winning their respective events. At Coronation, it had been Cindy's turn in the limelight with a narrow victory, her first-ever in barrel-racing.

Then, not to be outdone, C. J. had turned the trick at Wainwright with a win of his own. For C. J., his first-ever victory was especially sweet as the contestant he had beaten by just one point for the trophy buckle had been none other than Josh. He had been quick to point out to his cousin that this was just the first of many such victories to come.

Josh had good-naturedly pretended to be outraged

at being beaten. His performance earned him Jenny's "Miles Shivers Award," a huge bunch of very sour grapes.

With June having been a tremendously successful month for the quartet of youthful competitors, the Canadian standings were now dotted with D Lazy D names.

Josh was leading the Canadian standings in Steer Riding and C. J. was seventh, just one spot away from a Canadian Finals qualifying berth.

In Barrel Racing, Jenny was now among the top ten, sitting eighth in the standings while Cindy was in twelfth spot. She would need to climb at least two notches in the standings to earn the coveted trip to the Finals in Barrel Racing where there were ten finalists.

Still there was a lot of rodeo season left and not even those who were qualifying now could be assured of being there at season's end.

The Calgary Stampede, while it was only one rodeo, was one that could make or break cowboys and cowgirls vying for the CFR. Without a placing at Calgary, it would be very difficult to make the Finals for any of them except perhaps Josh, who was reasonably safe with his spot at the top of the Steer Riding standings.

Suddenly, a noise broke into C. J.'s dreamlike state of mind.

At first he was unable to place the sound. But there was something about it, something strange, something that didn't belong.

C. J. forced himself into total alertness. There it was again. It was a kind of a murmur. No, not a murmur; it was people talking.

But what was it that didn't fit? *That* was it, they weren't speaking English. It was a foreign language, a kind of guttural tongue that C. J. had heard before in movies about the Second World War.

He was about to call out a greeting, then checked himself. Instead, he very quietly jumped down from the chute and crouched down out of sight. Whoever was doing the talking was coming towards him.

C. J. peeked over the solid bottom portion of the chute gate and was only able to pick out two people approaching from out of the shadows. They were coming down the alleyway that ran under the infield bleachers.

From the way they were moving and the hushed tone of their voices, it seemed to C. J. that whoever the men were, they weren't interested in being seen by anyone else.

He wished they'd come a little closer or at least move out of the shadows so he could get a better look.

One of the men was doing most of the talking. He seemed quite excited and from time to time gestured in the direction of the camping area. It sounded as if he were giving the other man instructions.

At last, just as C. J. was becoming extremely uncomfortable in his crouched position and was beginning to think he'd soon have to move, the two men stepped out of the shadows and into the morning sunlight.

C. J. almost gasped out loud but was able to catch himself just in time. The first man, he was sure, was a stranger. But the other man, the one who had been doing all the talking, was someone he had seen before. That face and that frame C. J. would never forget.

There, not fifteen feet away from him, was the huge, brooding form of Baron Steg!

Chapter Twelve

C. J. had a decision to make!

Should he break and run and hope that Baron Steg and his crony would take long enough getting over the chute to allow him to escape? Or should he stay where he was, hoping not to be found out, and see if he could learn anything from the actions of the two men?

He quickly made up his mind. He would stay. He hunkered down still further behind the chute to avoid detection. The two men came closer, but fortunately for C. J., their attention was almost entirely focused on the camping area.

The boy could see the two men through the bars of the chute. Baron Steg's face was red and he appeared to be sweating, though the morning air still had a chill to it.

He's obviously worked up about something, C. J. thought to himself. They were close enough now that C. J. could almost reach out and touch the two men.

The huge Baron Steg continued to gesture excitedly and point towards the camping area. From time to time the other man nodded or responded with an incomprehensible sound, but otherwise said little.

Suddenly, something caught C. J.'s attention. From the stream of unintelligible words spewing from Baron Steg's mouth, came something that resembled the name "Douglas."

C. J. listened harder. There it was again – "Douglas." Then came another word that sounded like "Mendenstein." That was followed by a word he was sure was "Rolf." As Baron Steg spoke the name of the Prince, his face contorted with fury and he smashed a fist into the palm of his other hand.

Just then, another noise caught the attention of all three of them. From behind C. J. could be heard the distinct sound of approaching hoofbeats.

C. J. carefully manoeuvred himself so that he could see the rider. Across the arena he was able to distinguish the familiar form of Ben Bradley riding one horse and leading another. He obviously wanted to get an early start warming up his pickup horses.

Here was his chance. C. J. broke from his hiding place and sprinted as hard as he could toward Ben.

As Ben saw him coming, he started a wave of greeting, then held up as he realized C. J. was in a state of panic. The boy came up so fast, he startled Ben's horses and the cowboy had to bring them back under control.

"Sorry ... Ben," C. J. puffed excitedly. "It's Baron Steg and one of his men ... over there." He pointed to the area behind the chutes where he'd seen the two.

"Here, mount up!" Ben offered an arm and swung C. J. up onto the bare back of the second horse, a paint gelding.

Quickly he flipped the lead shank over the neck of the horse and fastened it to the halter to form a makeshift rein for C. J. "Let's go find out what those two birds are up to," Ben said. He kicked his horse into a lope, leaving C. J. behind for the moment.

The boy quickly caught up and pointed to the exact spot where he had overheard the conversation.

When they reached the front of the chutes, Ben swiftly dismounted and opened the gate to the centre alleyway that would be used to load the horses and bulls into the chutes for the Stampede.

Remounting, he led C. J. into the area behind the chutes.

"Right here?" Ben asked pointing to the place the two men had been standing.

"That's it," C. J. confirmed. "They were right there."

"Well, let's have a look around," Ben suggested.

Together, they rode up and down, combing the whole area behind the bucking chutes. They circled the pens that housed the rough stock out back and rode all the way to the race track and back into the infield.

Ben Bradley looked at C. J. and shrugged. "Beats me where they could have got to."

"It's like they just disappeared," C. J. agreed. "I can't figure it out. They were on foot and I didn't see any sign of a vehicle."

"Wait a minute!" Ben snapped his fingers. "There's one place we didn't look."

"Where's that?" C. J. asked the rugged cowboy.

"Right over there," Ben pointed.

"The tunnel!" C. J. exclaimed. "Of course, that's where they must have gone. But do you think they'd still be there?"

"It's worth checking out," Ben said and reined his mount around to head in the direction of the tunnel. C. J. followed quickly along.

The tunnel was just that. It was a long underground passageway that enabled contestants, officials, workmen and spectators to get to the infield area without having to cross the race track. The tunnel led from a point near the camping area down underground for a distance of probably one hundred metres, and emerged in the Stampede infield.

As the two riders arrived at the sloping ramp leading down into the tunnel, Ben pulled up his horse.

"C. J.," he spoke softly, "these guys mean business. Maybe you better wait here."

"No way, Ben," C. J. shook his head stubbornly. "If you're going down there, I'm going with you."

"All right, kid," Ben grinned at C. J. "I kind of figured you'd feel that way. Let's just take it real easy."

C. J. nodded grimly and side by side they walked their horses very deliberately down the ramp. Reaching the lower end of the ramp, they entered the tunnel.

As his tension increased, so did the level of C. J.'s

senses and he was especially alert to everything around him.

Though he had often walked through the tunnel, he had never looked at it as closely as he was right now.

The shod feet of the horses echoed like gunfire through the concrete tunnel. C. J. strained his eyes in an effort to see to the far end.

In the full light of day he would have been able to do so easily, but here in the early morning hours the opposite end of the tunnel hung in shadows.

In those shadows, C. J. was sure the Baron and his henchman were waiting, some kind of weapons in hand. He began to think he should have taken Ben's advice.

At about the halfway point, Ben held up a hand. They stopped, the sudden absence of sound almost as jarring as the pounding of the horse's hooves on the pavement had been.

Both cowboys strained to hear something ... *anything*. There was only silence.

Ben nodded and they resumed their slow nerve-wrenching march. As they neared the other end of the tunnel, light was beginning to filter into the entrance.

The last of the shadows were starting to dissolve into light. C. J. slowly blew air through tense lips as fear gave way to relief. There was no one there.

He turned to Ben Bradley. "Well I guess they're not... "

Ben suddenly grabbed C. J.'s arm. The boy stopped in mid-sentence. What was the noise? Ben wheeled his own horse around sharply, pulling C. J.'s paint around at the same time.

"Ride!" Ben screamed at C. J. as he slapped the paint hard with his open hand.

C. J. had no time to think. He dug his heels hard into the horse's sides, grabbed the mane with his free hand and hung on desperately.

Beside him he could hear and feel Ben Bradley galloping full out on his own horse and yelling loudly to get every last ounce of speed out of the two horses.

But it was neither the blast of hooves on pavement nor the wild hollering of Ben Bradley that had C. J.'s heart beating as if it would burst from the exertion.

The sound that terrified him was the sickening squeal of tires and the high-pitched roar of an engine behind them. The truck had to have been part-way up the other ramp; that was why they hadn't seen it.

Now it was closing fast on the two desperately fleeing riders!

Both C. J. and Ben knew that this was no scare tactic. They knew that if the truck and its occupants caught them, they would be run down without a thought.

C. J. bent low over the paint horse, hissing in his ear, while his feet never stopped flailing away at the animal's sides.

The ramp was just ahead. If only they could make it....

As C. J. and the paint hit the sunlight, the boy glanced back and realized he wouldn't make the top of the ramp. The truck was so close he could make out the evil faces of Baron Steg and his henchman who was behind the wheel.

Instinct took over. Whether it was his own idea or the horse acted out of its own fear, C. J. was never able to figure. But part-way up the ramp, the paint suddenly leaped high and to the right. C. J., riding bareback, almost fell off but was able to regain his balance.

The jump carried them off the ramp, over the concrete wall that lined it and to safety.

C. J. heard the pickup truck roar by him and at the same time heard the horrible scream of a horse in pain.

He jerked the paint to a stop and wheeled around. There, on the opposite side of the ramp, was Ben. He was on the ground trying to calm his terrified horse. The animal was rearing wildly.

At the top of the ramp, the truck had roared out into the infield, spun a 180 degree turn and stopped.

In the passenger seat, Baron Steg was glaring out at them. The driver was obviously waiting for instructions.

Ben was unable to bring his panic-stricken mount under control. The horse was still rearing and was in danger of falling back down onto the ramp. To avoid risking injury to his horse, Ben let him go and the frightened animal was off like a shot, giving vent to its panic in desperate out-of-control flight.

That left Ben helpless and on foot just yards away from the deadly Baron Steg.

C. J. saw Baron Steg's lips move and the driver of the truck threw it into gear. The vehicle began its deadly charge toward the unprotected cowboy.

A movement out of the corner of C. J.'s eye caught his attention. From the other side of the infield came the rumble of a semi-trailer truck. The huge liner with Roy Douglas grimly at the wheel and Jenny and Rolf alongside him on the seat and Josh standing on the passenger-side running board was moving fast. A huge cloud of dust was billowing skyward behind the truck as it bore down on the pickup truck of Baron Steg and his hood.

In the pickup, the two men were obviously unaware of what was taking place behind them. Their attention was solely and completely on Ben Bradley. The pickup gained speed and closed ground on Ben who was facing the deadly vehicle as it raced toward him.

At the last possible second, Ben dived to his left and the truck roared past, missing him by mere centimetres. Quickly Ben regained his feet as the driver of the pickup once again spun the vehicle in a half circle.

It was then that the two occupants of the pickup truck became aware of the liner catapulting toward them, its horn blaring and wheels churning waves of dust into the air behind it.

Baron Steg and his driver quickly lost interest in Ben Bradley. Spinning dust of their own, they veered the truck away from Ben and out of the path of the onrushing semi-trailer.

As the huge unit roared past Ben, he cheered and thrust a thumb into the air in a victory sign.

The pickup was much more manoeuvrable than the larger truck and easily got out of the way. Still the sight of several tons of cattle liner pelting towards them had clearly shaken the Baron and his driver.

Without even a backward glance to see what was

happening with the liner, the pickup raced into the tunnel. Seconds later, it emerged from the other end going at top speed and disappeared around the camping area and out of sight.

Ben Bradley jumped down onto the ramp, climbed up the other side and joined C. J. who was still holding onto the paint horse.

Ben grinned at the boy and took the halter shank in his own hand.

"Nothin' like a quiet ride before breakfast, eh kid?" he clapped C. J. on the back.

Roy Douglas had managed to get the cattle liner slowed down, turned around and now pulled alongside C. J. and Ben. The hiss of the air brakes accompanied the semi-trailer's coming to a stop.

Roy Douglas and his troupe of passengers climbed out of the rig and jumped down to where C. J., Ben and the paint were standing.

"Guess I don't have to ask who that was," Roy surmised, running a hand over his not-yet-shaven jaw.

"Baron Steg himself," C. J. replied.

"In the flesh," Ben added. "And I'll tell you somethin'. These boys aren't kiddin'' around. They're playin' hardball."

"They almost had us in the tunnel," C. J. explained vigorously. "My horse just jumped out of the way in time and ... by the way, what happened to you?" C. J. directed the question to Ben. "I thought they had you."

"So did I," Ben nodded solemnly. "I tried to do the same thing with my horse as you did, but he didn't quite make it.

"He went down hard on his knees but lucky for me, he cleared the wall," Ben went on. But with all the noise and the jump and the fall, he'd just about had it. He kind of went crazy there for a while.

"Speakin' of which," the pickup man pointed to where his horse was now grazing contentedly a couple of hundred metres away, "I better go fetch him."

As Ben sauntered off to collect his horse, C. J. related to the others the conversation he had overheard between the two villains, or at least the few snatches of it he understood.

"Well, it looks like we're back on full alert again," Roy Douglas said quietly.

"These men will stop at nothing to get at Rolf," he added pointedly. "And if any of us gets in their way, they won't hesitate to use whatever force is necessary to eliminate us.

"We'll have to be especially careful every moment from now on," he concluded.

Rolf looked down at the ground as he said, "I knew they were desperate men but I had no idea I would be putting all of you in so much danger. I'm sorry to be causing you so much trouble."

"Let's have no more of that kind of talk," Roy told him firmly. "We're in this together and we're just mighty glad to be of service to someone like you."

"Right!" Jenny chirped. "Just think, someday I'll be able to tell my kids that we helped the Crown Prince of Mendenstein overcome evil outlaws to gain his rightful place on the throne!" She gestured dramatically to make her point.

"Now *that's* a scary thought," Josh noted soberly.

"Josh, you aren't afraid of those evil outlaws, are you?" Jenny teased her brother.

"That's not what's scary," Josh replied with a chuckle. "I meant the thought of you having kids."

"Yeah, I know what you mean," C. J. joined in. "Can you imagine three or four little brats around, all like her?"

At that the two boys started back toward the camping area, both shaking their heads and continuing to exchange, in well-acted sombre tones, their deep distress at the notion that there might someday be offspring of Jenny's in this world.

Suddenly Rolf skipped off after them. "It's terrifying, that's what it is," he called loudly. "I mean, that red hair, that temper; I know what you guys mean."

With a sparkle in his eye, the Prince glanced over his shoulder at Jenny.

She was standing beside her father with her hands on her hips. Her freckled face was redder than usual, the result of a combination of anger and embarrassment.

She couldn't remain still any longer. "Creeps!" she shouted. "All of you ... creeps!"

She turned to her father. "There, that's better," she said in a businesslike tone of voice and started back toward the liner.

"Don't be upset, Jen," Roy Douglas told his feisty daughter. "I'm sure when you have children, they'll all be as sweet and gentle as you are."

Jenny looked quickly at him. Her father's face was a picture of innocence as he opened the door of the cab of the truck for her.

"Thank you," she said haughtily and climbed into the cab.

After closing the passenger side door, Roy Douglas jogged around to the other side of the cab and climbed in beside his daughter.

She watched him out of the corner of her eye. Suddenly, as if on cue, both of them broke into laughter. But even as they laughed, the question was uppermost in each of their minds: Where and when would Baron Steg and his men strike next?

Chapter Thirteen

"Yuk!" Jenny Douglas spat the word between bites of oatmeal and cornbread.

Across from her at the breakfast table, Laura Douglas looked up from her own breakfast. "Something the matter with the food, dear?"

"No, Mom," Jenny replied quickly, "the food's fine. It's just ... it's just that the thought of Miles Shivers winning the Steer Riding at the Calgary Stampede makes me want to be... sick."

"I know what you mean, Jen," her father nodded in agreement. "Not only that, but if Lefty Shivers can ride Bad Medicine today, he could win the fifty thousand dollars. How do you like that possibility?"

"Yuk!" Jenny repeated, tossing her red hair violently from side to side.

"That about sums it up all right," Josh added ruefully.

"Well, I've got news for you," C. J. spoke up resolutely, "I'm not going to let Miles Shivers win the Steer Riding." He paused and looked around the motorhome. "I'm going to win it," he announced in a hushed voice.

"That's the spirit!" Rolf offered encouragingly.

"Well," Roy Douglas smiled at his nephew, "you're the only one who can stop him now."

It was true. After nine days of the Stampede, there had been several surprises.

Josh, the defending Stampede champion, had failed to qualify for the final day of competition. His first steer had been a bad draw and the young cowboy had been able to muster only 53 points on the animal.

Even coupled with a 70-point score on his second steer, the result wasn't good enough to earn Josh the right to ride in the championship round.

Equally surprising was the identity of the leader after the first two steers – Miles Shivers! The younger of the Shivers boys had always been talented enough, but in the past had always let his own bad attitude stand in the way of success.

At this year's Stampede, however, Miles had settled down to attempt what had previously eluded him: the winning of a major championship. And with the exception of the Canadian championship, no title was more prestigious than that of the Calgary Stampede.

Equally surprising was the performance of Miles' brother Lefty, who had made it to the Finals in the Bull Riding.

In the five major events of rodeo, of which Bull Riding was one, the day's reward was an incredible fifty thousand dollars per event. Five cowboys would walk away from the rodeo arena fifty thousand dollars richer, making a grand total of one quarter of a million dollars that was to be paid out during the course of that afternoon.

The fourth surprise also involved the Shivers boys. Despite the fact that they had obviously been around for the entire Stampede, their paths had not once crossed those of anyone from the D Lazy D.

In fact, it almost seemed that the villainous pair were going out of their way to avoid confrontations with any of the Douglas Rodeo outfit.

While all were relieved at this unexpected turn of events, they were waiting expectantly. Something had to happen.

Nine days and not a whit of trouble. There hadn't even been any sign of Baron Steg or any of his gang since the wild incident of the first morning of Stampede. As per Roy Douglas' instructions, each of the D Lazy D crew had been particularly careful throughout the nine days of Stampede already completed.

The watch over Rolf had been doubled. Now, whenever possible, he went nowhere without at least two companions.

Still, all was quiet. There had been no sign of anything unusual ... and that in itself was scary.

Jenny had protested many times that "things are *too* quiet around here; I don't like it."

With the Stampede into its last day, however, attention was on the excitement of C. J.'s chances for a championship and whether or not Lefty Shivers could get by the rank Douglas bull, Bad Medicine. The Douglas outfit relaxed their guard just a little.

At least one point was in their favor. With both Miles and Lefty Shivers in the Stampede Finals, the two brothers would have little time to engage in any skullduggery.

The final surprise was perhaps the biggest. C. J., only a steer rider for a little over a year, had wound up second to Miles Shivers after the first two steers of the Stampede. He had the best chance, if anyone did, of catching Miles on that final day.

The final day of the Stampede usually involved a great deal of turmoil for everyone involved.

This year was no different. Roy Douglas gulped his breakfast down and rushed off to join Ben Bradley and Len Tucker at the stock pens.

The stock scheduled for use that day had to be cut out and placed in separate pens, equipment had to be readied and finally the men themselves would be taking extra pains to spruce themselves up.

The last performance of the Stampede demanded that everyone look his best, both for the live crowd and for television.

Jenny and Cindy headed off to tend their horses. Jenny's barrel racing horse, Sugar, had strained a tendon when she slipped going round the third barrel during Jenny's first run at the Stampede.

The injury had put an end to Jenny's chances for a Stampede championship.

Of more concern was the fact that Sugar was lame, although the vet had indicated the injury was not serious.

Because Josh's help was needed behind the chutes and C. J. was riding in the Finals, Jenny and Cindy were assigned the task of staying close to Rolf for the afternoon.

For the time being, however, the young Prince stayed at the motorhome, assisting Laura Douglas with the cleanup after breakfast.

The morning passed quickly, and as the afternoon sun spread its generous warmth over the Stampede grandstand and the enormous crowd that filled it, rodeo time arrived.

The Bareback Riding and Steer Wrestling event came and went amidst thunderous roaring from the crowd for winners and losers alike.

As the time approached for the start of the Boys Steer Riding, Josh and C. J. were behind the chutes. C. J. had done up, then undone his chaps at least twenty times.

He'd warmed up his rope, put on his gloves, checked his spurs to make sure the rowels were free of obstruction and adjusted his hat. He had repeated that process in that exact same sequence over and over for the past half hour.

"You are driving me nuts," Josh groaned. "Will you just relax?"

"Right, you're right!" C. J. agreed. "That's what I have to do ... relax. There's nothing to worry about. It's just another steer ... just another ride ... right? Just have to relax."

He began warming his rope one more time.

"Will you quit that please?" Josh demanded of his cousin. "The rope's ready ... everything's ready . . . you're ready!"

Then they heard announcer Hank Parker over the Stampede's powerful sound system: "Looks like the steers are in for the start of the Boys Steer Riding."

"C'mon," said Josh and took C. J.'s trembling arm. "This is it. It's time to do your stuff."

C. J. swallowed and nodded grimly. There wasn't a cowardly bone in the body of this transplant from Eastern Canada, but as he heard Hank Parker's call to the Steer Riding contestants, his palms became instantly sweaty, his legs lost their will to hold him up and he was shaking to such an extent that he dropped his rope.

Josh picked it up. He knew that it was best to move quickly and get C. J. on his steer with as little delay as possible. The longer they took, the more nervous his cousin was sure to become.

C. J. would be second last out, just before Miles Shivers.

The first four riders were quickly out of the chutes. Two of the boys bucked off and the other two made qualified rides with scores in the low sixties.

None of those results would likely have any impact on either C. J. or Miles. It would boil down to what each of them could do ... a head-to-head showdown.

C. J. eased down on his steer. Roy Douglas was alongside him in the chute. Josh was up on the back of the chute helping his cousin with his preparations.

None of them spoke a word. As C. J. took his final wrap, Josh patted him encouragingly on the back and Roy Douglas winked his own wish for good luck.

C. J. nodded and the gate swung open. The steer started slowly. Its first couple of jumps were easy to handle. Then the animal seemed to shift into high gear, leaping high, twisting in mid-air and crashing down hard on its front legs.

C. J., his teeth gritted and his chest thrust out, weathered the storm. He knew that if he made one mistake he'd be flat on his back in the Stampede topsoil.

Two more routine jumps and there it was − the welcome sound of the eight-second whistle. C. J. quickly made his dismount. He raised his arms over his head and gratefully accepted the appreciative salute of the crowd.

As he walked back to the chutes, he knew he'd been good enough to beat any of the riders who had been out so far.

Still, he had come into the Finals two points back of Miles Shiver and desperately needed a big score to win.

The voice of Hank Parker came over the P.A. system – "72 points for C. J. Findlay!" the announcer informed the crowd.

C. J. wasn't sure if he was happy with the score or not.

75 points would certainly have been better. Miles would need only 70 points to tie and 71 to win the title and, although C. J. disliked Miles Shivers about as much as it is possible to dislike anybody, he had to admit that the younger half of the Shivers boys was a very capable steer rider.

As he arrived back at the chutes, C. J. received congratulations from Josh, Jenny, Cindy and Rolf. All four had been perched on the back of the chute for C. J.'s all-important ride.

"Good ride."

"Great show."

"Good job."

"Nice goin', C. J."

"I don't know," C. J. responded slowly as he coiled up his bull rope. "I'm not sure that's going to be enough points."

They wouldn't have to wait long. The chute gate swung open and Miles Shivers was in the arena on the back of a very athletic, tawny-coloured steer.

He was sitting perfectly in the middle of the steer's back and jabbing his heels energetically into the steer's sides. Miles Shivers made it look easy. He even stepped off at the end of his ride rather than throwing himself off.

Then he thrust his fist into the air in a cocky victory salute. There was a grotesque sneer on the steer rider's face when he turned to face the chutes and he repeated the gesture with his fist.

"Rather arrogant chap, isn't he?" Rolf remarked.

"He's a creep!" Cindy corrected him.

"Look at him," Jenny added. "Doesn't he make you want to..."

She was interrupted by Hank Parker's voice.

"Here it is, folks," the announcer told the crowd, "it's official; our Calgary Stampede champion steer rider with that 73-point ride is Miles Shivers."

C. J. turned away from the infield and climbed silently back behind the chutes.

He was quickly surrounded by his friends, all of them sharing his disappointment.

"Don't feel bad," Josh told him. "You made a heck of a ride. He just had a better steer than you did."

"You'll beat him next time," Jenny said confidently.

"That's right," Rolf chimed in. "You'll kick his arrogant butt next time."

Everyone looked at the Prince in surprise.

"You know, I believe your language is deteriorating on the rodeo circuit," said Jenny, looking accusingly at him.

Rolf tried to suppress a smile when he said, "You're right, of course... I should have said 'you'll rise to the occasion next opportunity, old boy.'"

C. J. didn't feel much like joining in the fun that he knew was for his benefit. "I really wanted to win. Not just to beat Miles. I would have loved to win at the Calgary Stampede," he spoke softly.

"Do you know how many people have never even been second at the Calgary Stampede?" Jenny pointed out.

"And don't forget," Josh noted, "winning second here puts you into the top six in Canada. If you can hold on, you'll be at the Canadian Finals."

"And so will Miles Shivers," Jenny added.

"That's where you can kick his butt!" Rolf cried excitedly.

"Oops," he said ruefully when he realized what he'd said.

Cindy stepped forward and softly placed a kiss on C. J.'s cheek.

"You're a champion to me, Calgary Stampede or not," she told him gently.

Instantly there were cries of "Hubba hubba," "Ooh la la," and "Look at the lovebirds" from the other three.

C. J. responded by sticking out his tongue at his tormentors. Then, arm in arm with Cindy, he headed off in the direction of the refreshment stand.

Chapter Fourteen

It was soon time for the bull riding and all of the Douglas Rodeo crew were nervous. It was bad enough that Miles Shivers had won the Steer Riding but if his older brother were to ride Bad Medicine and win the bull riding, that would be more than any of them could stand.

Shivers had met up with Bad Medicine twice before and the result had been the same both times.

The bull had easily bested the cowboy, to the great delight of everyone at the D Lazy D.

In fact, Bad Medicine had only been ridden once ever. That was by Len Tucker when he had made his farewell ride the year before.

As the time came for the matchup between the

villainous cowboy and the ill-natured bull, the D Lazy D outfit gathered together to watch.

Len Tucker and Ben Bradley, who were picking up, rode over to the spot where everyone was congregated near the bucking chutes.

"What do you think, Len?" Josh asked. "Can he ride 'im?"

"I don't know," Len replied slowly. "Much as I hate to admit it, Shivers has a lot of talent and the guts of a burglar. If he can... If he can get by the first three jumps or so, he'll have a chance."

From where they were they could see Lefty Shivers warming his rope while sitting on the bull's back.

Bad Medicine was docile in the chute, almost as if he realized he should be saving his energy for the eight seconds in the arena.

Lefty Shivers took his final wrap, then slapped his face a couple of times, a common practice among bullriders as they psyched themselves up for the impending danger.

"I wish he'd let me do that," Jenny grumbled to no one in particular.

At that moment the gate opened and Bad Medicine was airborne. His first jump was so high that daylight could be seen between his belly and the top of the chutes.

The mighty bull crashed down hard, every ounce of his eighteen hundred pounds intent on freeing itself of the unwanted rider.

The bull spun hard to the left, leaping high at the same time. Now the combination of downdraft and centrifugal force was causing Lefty some problems.

The bull rider was tipped forward and to one side. In an unbelievable display of athletic ability the bull then reversed the direction of his spin.

Now he was whirling hard to the right. Lefty Shivers had no chance. But what was worse, he fell "into the well," meaning that his body was on the inside and directly in the path of the spinning bull.

The first time the bull came around, the rider was crashed brutally to the arena ground. Stunned and helpless, Lefty Shivers was sure to be trampled the next time the bull spun around.

At just that moment the surprisingly swift figure of Tub Willoughby appeared as if from nowhere.

With his hand right on the bull's nose, the diminutive bullfighter got the animal's attention. Bad Medicine followed the gaudily clad clown away from the downed cowboy, his enormous feet missing the prostrate bullrider by mere centimetres.

The crowd had been holding its breath as the drama involving Shivers unfolded.

Now, as the courage and daring of the rodeo clown saved the cowboy, twenty-five thousand people rose as one. Their salute to Tub Willoughby, who capped it all off by dancing neatly away from Bad Medicine's menacing horns, lasted for at least thirty seconds.

"Wow," breathed C. J., "that was close."

"For a minute there, I thought he was a dead duck," Jenny noted. "I couldn't decide whether I was glad or worried about the creep."

Josh laughed. "Well, thanks to Tub, Lefty's all right. I can see him from here."

"Mr. Willoughby was positively magnificent," Rolf enthused.

"Hey, you wanna meet him?" Jenny asked.

"That would be great!" Rolf exclaimed.

"The bull riding's just about over," Jenny told him. "We'll go over to his trailer and I'll introduce you to him.

"But you better not call him Mister Willoughby," she went on with a chuckle. "He won't know who you're talking to."

"Hey, don't forget what Dad said," Josh warned. "We're supposed to stay close. You never know who might be..."

"Tub's trailer is just over there," Jenny scoffed, pointing to the area behind the chutes. "You can practically see it from here."

With that, she was off. Rolf, happy to be free for the moment, scurried after her.

It would take Tub a few minutes to get back to his trailer, so Jenny and the Prince stopped off on the way for an ice cream. Both of them were brimming with excitement from the events of the day.

Ice cream in hand, they meandered slowly in the direction of Tub Willoughby's trailer.

"What's Mendenstein like?" Jenny asked the young Prince.

"Well," Rolf began slowly, "it's much like parts of your country.

"When we passed through the Rockies on our way to and from Vancouver, I was most reminded of my country. The palace where my father and I live... "

"You live in a palace?" Jenny interrupted him.

"Yes, of course," Rolf nodded. "It's located high up in a mountain pass. The city is surrounded by alpine meadows.

"Many mornings there are wild animals right on the grounds of the palace as I look out my window."

"What sort of wild animals?" Jenny asked.

"Well, there are..."

"Shhh!!" Jenny suddenly clapped a hand over Rolf's mouth.

They were alongside Tub's trailer. The rodeo clown was nowhere to be seen.

Jenny dropped to her knees and pulled the Prince down beside her.

Rolf yanked her hand away from his mouth. "What do you think you're... "

Jenny silenced the outraged Prince a second time, employing the same method she had the first time.

"Shhh!" she repeated in an excited whisper. "Listen!!" Removing her hand from Rolf's mouth, Jenny strained to hear. Rolf, realizing she wasn't joking, did the same.

There it was. They both knew it immediately. From the other side of the trailer came the unmistakable voice of Baron Steg!

Jenny and Rolf listened in horror. Steg was speaking English but it was difficult to pick out the words.

Then another man was speaking. He was a little easier to understand. "... on their way over here to see Willoughby. We can grab 'em when they get here."

Jenny recognized the speaker. The voice was that of Lefty Shivers. He must have either overheard or got wind of their plans to stop by Tub's trailer.

"C'mon, we'll just wait right here for them," Lefty Shivers could be heard telling Baron Steg.

"They're coming this way," Jenny hissed at Rolf.

She looked around frantically. There was no one around to help them. They had to do something!

There, in front of them, was Tub's clown barrel. Quickly, Jenny gestured to Rolf that she wanted him to climb inside.

Holding his ice cream, she clumsily assisted the Prince up and into the barrel, then pushed his head down to force him to duck down.

Reaching down inside, she handed the two ice cream cones to Rolf, then hoisted herself up and into the barrel. There was barely room for the two of them to squish down inside.

They held their breath as they heard Baron Steg and Lefty Shivers come around the corner of the trailer.

The two criminals stopped right beside the barrel and resumed their conversation.

"By the way, when do I get my money?" Shivers asked.

"You'll get your money when you have delivered the goods," the heavily accented voice of Baron Steg replied. "I make it a practice of making sure the job is completed before I pay anyone five thousand dollars."

Inside the barrel, Jenny and Rolf looked quickly at each other.

"Don't worry," Lefty Shivers was replying, "you'll get the kid, no problem."

Jenny snuck a peek up at the top of the barrel. What she saw caused the hair on the back of her neck to stand on end.

Lefty Shivers was leaning on the barrel as he talked to Baron Steg! Jenny could have reached up and touched his elbow.

At that moment a third voice could be heard. Someone else had joined the two unpleasant characters. "What can I do for you boys?" Jenny and Rolf heard the newest voice ask.

Jenny recognized the high-pitched drawl of Tub Willoughby.

"Not a thing, Tub," Lefty replied. "We're just waiting here for a couple of friends of ours."

"Oh, well, sure ain't no law against waitin'," Tub answered cordially. "You recovered from your wreck out there in the arena?"

"Sure I'm fine," Lefty said, but he didn't sound very happy.

"Wasn't much of a wreck anyway," he went on. "That sorry bull of Douglas's was just lucky."

"Right," Tub could be heard to say in an exaggerated manner. "Excuse me."

Jenny guessed that the "excuse me" meant Tub was going by the two other men. She crossed her fingers that Tub wasn't about to leave.

Suddenly she was struck in the face by a very sweaty and outlandishly coloured shirt. The force of the blow knocked her ice cream into her chin.

She had barely time to recover before a bright red fright wig struck Rolf directly on top of the head. The boy was so surprised he dropped his ice cream cone in Jenny's lap.

What was going on anyway? She peeked up at the opening of the barrel.

Lefty's arm was no longer leaning on the barrel. She could just make out the form of Tub Willoughby removing his makeup with paper towels. She was furious. "That stupid clown is throwing his dirty clothes in here," she thought to herself.

As he finished with each paper towel, Tub deposited that too into the barrel and onto the hapless refugees inside. In her fury, Jenny lost track of the conversation that was taking place outside. She was about to stand up, poke her head out of the barrel and give Tub Willoughby a piece of her mind, Baron Steg or no Baron Steg.

At that moment, what was being said outside caught her attention again. Tub was talking.

"Y'know Lefty, I can sure understand why you cain't hardly stand those Douglas kids," he drawled, discarding another soiled towel into the barrel.

"Is that so?" Lefty Shivers grunted in reply.

"Yep, I sure can," Tub continued. "Why, just now I was talking to that pain-in-the-patoot daughter of theirs, you know the one with that stringy red hair and all..."

"Wait a minute," Lefty interrupted. "You were talking to her ... when?"

"Just now," Tub responded. "Her and that weird little brat with the funny accent."

"Where?" Lefty grabbed his arm. "Where were you talkin' to them?"

"Oh, I ran into 'em on my way over here," Tub droned on. "They was headed for the midway and then they was gonna help their pa get loaded up for the trip home."

"Uh, look ... uh ... Tub ... it looks like our friends ain't gonna get over this way after all," Lefty stammered. "I guess we'll be goin'."

"Gee, what's your hurry?" Tub was whining now. "You never even introduced me to your friend."

If there was a reply, Jenny and Rolf couldn't hear it from inside the barrel.

Suddenly, without warning, the barrel was turned sharply on its side. It was being rolled and bounced over the rough ground.

Inside, Jenny and Rolf were being tossed around like socks in a dryer. Their plight was made all the worse by the fact that bouncing around with them were ice cream, sweaty clothes and makeup-stained paper towels.

At last, after what seemed an endless journey, the barrel was stopped and righted. Still, the two occupants of the barrel made no sound.

"Okay, you can come out now," they heard Tub Willoughby say.

They dared not answer.

"It's okay I said." Tub looked into the barrel. "They've gone."

Slowly and gingerly, Jenny climbed out of the cramped barrel. She looked quickly around. Tub was telling the truth. There was no one else in sight.

Rolf followed her out of the barrel.

Tub Willoughby began to laugh, softly at first, then harder until finally he was laughing so hard, tears were streaming down his face.

"What's so funny?" Jenny demanded.

"You... you should... see yourselves." The rodeo clown had trouble getting the words out through his laughter.

Jenny and Rolf looked at one another. Tub had a point.

Their clothes were a mess. Their hair and faces were generously splotched with ice cream. One of the cones had lodged itself in Jenny's red hair.

Slowly, smiles spread over the smeared faces of the two barrel stowaways.

"Hey, wait a minute," Jenny suddenly shook an accusing finger at Tub Willoughby. "You knew we were in there all the time, didn't you?"

"Sure I did," Tub acknowledged with a grin.

"Then what was the idea of throwing all that junk in there?" Jenny's eyes were blazing.

"Well," Tub explained in his slow drawl, "I also figured you didn't really want to be found by Lefty and his large friend.

"So I figured I'd divert their attention away from the barrel by using it like a garbage can. People don't usually like to hang around other people's garbage and dirty laundry.

"Makes sense, don't it?" Tub asked with a sly wink at Rolf.

"It makes sense to me, Mr. Willoughby," Rolf agreed readily.

"Well," said Jenny, not totally convinced, "well... well you didn't have to enjoy it so much. And what's this about stringy hair?"

"Sorry, I couldn't resist," Tub laughed loudly as he tossed them each a towel.

"Look," he suddenly became serious, "it's none of my business, but I wouldn't mess around with those two if I were you."

"Believe me," Rolf replied. "We'd rather not."

Tub Willoughby nodded, then laughed again as he

watched Jenny trying to repair the damage to her appearance.

"Still friends?" he asked her mischievously.

"I dunno," Jenny hesitated. "Well, I guess so," she laughed at last and tossed the towel in Tub's face.

"Come on Rolf," she ordered the Prince. "Dad's gonna be mad enough already for me letting us get into this jam. Let's hurry back to the motorhome before we get in any more trouble."

"So long, Tub," she called as she hurried away.

"Nice meeting you, Mr. Willoughby," Rolf called as he hustled after her.

As they looked back, they could see Tub looking behind and under things. They could hear him muttering to himself, "Where's this Mr. Willoughby anyway?"

Chapter Fifteen

What followed the conclusion to the Calgary Stampede had been three of the busiest days in the lives of every member of the Douglas Rodeo outfit, for three days was all the time there was before the start of the long trip to Toronto.

The stock had been transported back to the D Lazy D and put out to pasture for a much-needed few days of green grass before the lengthy journey over the Trans-Canada.

Chores had had to be done and the ranch made

ready to run virtually on its own for ten days. All of the paperwork associated with the end of the Stampede and the start of another rodeo had had to be looked after.

Clothes were unpacked, washed and repacked, boots polished, hats cleaned, damaged equipment repaired and vehicles carefully serviced.

Roy Douglas spent hours on the phone making arrangements to unload, feed and water the stock at points along the way.

And somehow, perhaps because they really had no choice, they made it. Everything was done at the ranch and all the preparations for the all-important trip East were completed.

And right on schedule the caravan bearing the familiar signage of the Douglas Rodeo Outfit pulled away from the D Lazy D.

And now, four days after setting out from the little ranch in the foothills of Alberta, the exhausted band of travellers was nearing its destination.

C. J.'s pulse began to quicken from the time he was first able to spot the CN Tower needling its way skyward over a sprawling, pre-dawn Toronto.

The excitement of the boy's return to his hometown had become evident about the time the convoy of rodeo vehicles crossed the border into Ontario two mornings earlier.

Up to that point, in recognition of his homeward journey, C. J. had been occupying the place of honor in the passenger seat of the first liner. However, as his chatter increased to the point of being non-stop, even the easy-going Ben Bradley could stand it no more.

Three hours into the mammoth Laurentian Shield of Ontario, Ben called over the CB that the caravan would have to stop.

Slowly the big trucks lumbered to a halt. Ben, offering the excuse that it was only fair that C. J.'s unceasing talk about the city of his birth be shared with everyone, negotiated a trade. One C. J. for one Josh and a Prince.

Undaunted, C. J. bounced happily up alongside his Uncle Roy and resumed his chatter, with only a slight pause to catch his breath.

By lunchtime, Roy Douglas knew the batting averages of every man who had ever worn a Toronto Blue Jays' uniform as well as the names of all of the stops on the Yonge - University line of the Metro Toronto Rapid Transit System. He had listened to a detailed description of every exhibit in the Ontario Science Centre (there were over eight hundred, he was assured!) and had become acquainted with most of the displays in the Hockey Hall of Fame and all ninety-eight rooms of Casa Loma.

C. J.'s next verbal tour was to be that of the Royal Ontario Museum. However, when C. J. led off with the information that there were some six million treasures in this respectable facility, Roy Douglas decided it was time for lunch.

After the lunch break, C. J. had been shifted one place further back. Len Tucker was his next victim.

By supper time that evening C. J. was in the motorhome with Laura Douglas, Jenny and Cindy McKannin. They seemed best equipped to handle the gregarious Torontonian – Mrs. Douglas with her never-ending patience, and Jenny and Cindy with their walkmans.

Now, as the city's skyline was finally coming into view, C. J. had been allowed to return to his spot in the lead truck.

This time, however, Ben Bradley was ready. He had borrowed a walkman from the sympathetic Jenny. Though he was a die-hard country music fan, Ben had gratefully accepted Jenny's offer of a Bon Jovi tape and had listened to both sides three times.

In truth, all of them shared C. J.'s excitement. For all but Roy and Laura, who had been there some ten years before, the trip to Toronto was a first.

And, despite their good-natured grumbling, each appreciated, at least a little, C. J.'s well-meaning explanations about the place.

Arrangements had been made at the Canadian National Exhibition Grounds to house the livestock, so that was the first stop once inside the city.

Now C. J.'s value to the expedition was felt. With him giving directions, there was no need for road maps.

In no time, the stock was unloaded, fed, watered and bedded down. There was even time to saddle up Doc Holliday and Sugar for a brief jaunt around the exhibition grounds. The horses enjoyed the opportunity to get the kinks out, even though they had been frequently unloaded and exercised during the four-day trip to Toronto.

Jenny's mare, Sugar, seemed fully recovered from her injury and would likely be ready to race at the Toronto rodeo.

C. J. sat tall and straight on the ebony back of Doc Holliday and pointed out a couple of landmarks to Jenny.

Now that he was actually in Toronto, the boy was much more subdued, his excitement having been replaced by a kind of relaxed contentment.

"I can't believe it," he told Jenny with a shake of his head. "I've been to the C.N.E. every year since I could walk, except last year when I was with you guys out west. I've probably walked these grounds a hundred times, maybe two hundred. But I never thought someday I'd be riding around here, on my own horse, my own wild black stallion."

C. J. reached down and gave Doc Holliday an affectionate pat on his well-muscled neck.

"Yeah, it's all been a big change for you, hasn't it?" Jenny remarked.

C. J. looked at his cousin. "You know, as much as I've loved rodeo and being a part of your way of life, I guess this will always be my home," he said thoughtfully. "I guess I'd always come back here in the end."

Jenny nodded. "I can understand that; home is home and that never changes," she said solemnly.

It was the first time in a long time C. J. and his

high-spirited cousin had had a serious conversation. C. J. was seeing a softer side of Jenny, a side he had forgotten was there.

"What do you want to do ... you know ... when ... " Jenny fumbled for words.

"When I grow up?" C. J. filled in with a laugh.

"Yeah, I guess that's what I mean," Jenny acknowledged with a grin.

"That's easy. I'm planning to be an architect. I want to design big buildings ... like those." C. J. pointed to the spires of downtown Toronto.

He was about to explain the excitement he imagined would come from creating these man-made wonders when something caught his eye. Off to their right, tucked between two older C.N.E. buildings, was a pickup truck – one that C. J. was sure he had seen before.

"Keep looking straight ahead," he said quietly. "I think we're being watched."

"Are you kidding?" Jenny asked incredulously.

"I'm not sure, but that looks like Baron Steg's pickup truck over there to our right," he breathed.

Casually, C. J. and Jenny angled the horses in such a way as to get a better look at the suspicious vehicle without appearing to do so.

Then they made a wide, unhurried circle and headed back in the direction of the rest of the Douglas outfit.

"That's it all right!" Jenny exclaimed as soon as they were turned away from the truck. "But how could they have known where we'd be and when we'd get here?"

"I don't know," C. J. shrugged. "Maybe they just guessed. Let's work around behind them and see if we can get a look at who's there," he suggested.

"Well ... okay," Jenny agreed reluctantly, "but not too close. Those guys don't mess around."

Doing their best to look casual and unhurried, Jenny and C. J. guided their mounts toward a narrow alleyway between two buildings. Reaching the passage which was out of sight of the pickup truck, they spurred their horses into a gallop, circled around the building and came out a couple of hundred metres behind the truck.

Quickly they dismounted and tied the horses to a couple of posts. Then, using doorways, large garbage disposal containers and parked vehicles for cover, they zigzagged a path until they were close enough to get a look at the occupants of the truck.

There was Lefty Shivers propped against the fender of the truck. He was peering intently across the grounds through a pair of binoculars. His younger brother Miles was perched on the hood of the truck.

Less than fifty metres separated Jenny and C. J. from the Shivers boys.

C. J. peeked out of the doorway in which they had taken refuge. He could see that Miles and Lefty were conversing, but couldn't make out what was being said. "Let's get a little closer," he whispered to Jenny. "I want to hear what they're saying."

"What about Baron Steg?" Jenny asked.

"He must not be around," C. J. assured her. "Come on."

"I hope you're right." Jenny crossed her fingers as they dashed to another doorway just a few metres from the back of the pickup. Now they could clearly hear what was being said.

"Where did those two get to?" Miles was asking his brother.

"Dunno," came the reply. "They disappeared around the corner. Doesn't matter. It ain't them we're interested in anyway."

"Can you see what's goin' on with the rest of them?" Miles asked with a loud yawn.

"They're just about finished with the stock," Lefty growled his reply. "They'll probably head out right after those other two punks get back."

"What do we do then?" came Miles nasal whine.

"We follow 'em," said Lefty as he flashed his brother an unpleasant grin. "Shouldn't be too hard now."

Both of them laughed loudly. "I gotta admit," Miles slapped his leg with glee, "buggin' their motorhome with that microphone was one of the best ideas yet."

"Yeah," Lefty agreed readily. "Makes it awful easy to keep track of 'em don't it? One thing I'll say about ol' Baron Steg ... he does provide the latest in technological advances."

The two brothers laughed again. "Yep," Lefty went on, "we just keep listenin' in and that yappy redhead is sure to tell us everythin' we want to know. Then, first time they leave our royal friend alone ... zap! ... we move in, put the grab on him and just like that, we're ten thousand dollars richer."

"Ten?" Miles whistled. "I thought it was only five thousand."

"That was before," Lefty winked at him. "But your crafty ol' brother did a little renegotiatin' with our friend Baron Steg. Now that there's only a few days left until the big deadline, I figured our price ought to go up a little bit."

"I dunno, Lefty," Miles said slowly. "That Baron guy scares me. And those friends of his ... they're even worse. If we mess this up..."

"Shut up," Lefty growled. "We ain't gonna mess up nothin'.

"All we gotta do is grab the kid, hand him over to the Baron and collect the cash." He snapped his fingers to emphasize his point.

"What... what do ya think they'll do to 'im?" Miles asked carelessly.

"Who cares!" was Lefty's off-handed reply. "Ain't no skin off our noses what happens to the phony little creep."

"Ya think he's a real Prince?" Miles asked his brother.

"Well, if he is, he won't be for long." Lefty threw back his head and emitted a long, evil laugh.

In their hiding place, C. J. and Jenny both shivered involuntarily. C. J. gave a signal that Jenny was to follow and quickly the pair retraced the zig-zag path back to the horses. Silently they mounted up and started back to where everyone was waiting for them and probably beginning to wonder where they were.

Neither of them said a word for the first while. Each was deep in horrified thought at what might happen to Rolf if he were taken by the Shivers boys.

At last, certain they were out of hearing range of the two vicious brothers, Jenny could contain herself no longer.

"Those creeps," she fumed, "if they get their hands on the Prince..." She was so angry she couldn't finish the thought.

"Well, at least we know how they figured out where we'd be and when," C. J. noted.

"Come on, let's get back to the motorhome," Jenny said determinedly and kicked Sugar into a trot. "I want to find that bug thing and get rid of it."

As they had suspected, there was a definite air of impatience when they got back.

"Where've you been?" Roy Douglas asked. "We were getting worried. We were just going to start looking for you."

"We're being spied on," Jenny blurted.

She started to point in the direction of the Shivers boys but C. J. stopped her.

"Don't point," he told her.

"They're watching us with field glasses. They're across the grounds behind us."

"Look towards those grey buildings all in a row straight behind me. They're hidden between two of them," he directed his Uncle Roy.

"Not only that, but our motorhome's bugged," Jenny fumed as she climbed down from Sugar's back.

"How do you know?" Josh asked, his eyes wide.

"We sneaked up on them and overheard what they were talking about," Jenny explained with a grin.

"They got some kind of a bug from Baron Steg and somehow hooked it up in the motorhome," C. J. explained as he began uncinching Doc Holliday.

"What's a bug?" Rolf's high-pitched voice asked.

"A microphone," Roy Douglas explained. "By hiding it inside the motorhome they are able to listen in on some kind of receiver they probably have in their pickup. They can hear everything anyone says in the motorhome and that way they can be one step ahead of us."

"They said something about some redhead that would blab everything they needed to know," said C. J., who couldn't help getting in a dig at his cousin.

Jenny rose to the bait, "Hah," she responded with an angry kick at the pavement, "I'll show those jerks. I'm going to find that microphone and rip it out."

She stomped off in the direction of the motorhome.

"Wait a minute, Jen," Roy Douglas caught his daughter's arm, "let's not be in too much of a hurry to pull that thing out of there. We might just be able to use their little device to our advantage."

"How?" Jenny demanded.

"Well," her father explained patiently, "now that we know it's there, we can make sure those boys only hear what we want them to hear."

"Hey, I get it!" Josh clapped his hands together. "We can feed them some wrong information and maybe get them out of our hair."

"Right," his father replied. "Now let's put these horses away and find out exactly where that bug is."

It was while he was bedding down Doc Holliday in his box stall that C. J. devised a plan.

Chapter Sixteen

"Casa Loma!" C. J. exclaimed, with a glance over his shoulder to make sure they were far enough away from the motorhome so that there was no chance he could be heard.

"Oh no," Jenny groaned, "not another one of your guided tours."

"No, listen!" C. J. told her impatiently. "I know that place like the back of my hand.

"If we can use the bug in the motorhome to lure the Shivers boys up there ... well, I think we could come up with a Toronto surprise or two." He rubbed his hands together gleefully.

"What exactly is Casa Loma, anyway?" Rolf asked.

"Oh no," Jenny clapped a hand over the Prince's

mouth in mock horror, "now you've done it; he'll be giving us a three-hour explanation."

"It's a castle," C. J. told Rolf, ignoring Jenny's remark. "There are ninety-eight rooms in all and a few places that just might fit into our plans very nicely."

"It wouldn't, by any chance, have a dungeon, would it?" Rolf inquired, a sly grin spreading over his features.

"Actually, no," C. J. replied, shaking his head. "There's no dungeon in Casa Loma. This castle was built in the early part of this century. Dungeons were kind of out of style by then.

"It's a museum now and what it has got is secret passages, lots of places to hide and a couple of spots to get somebody very lost."

"Like the Shivers boys?" Jenny raised her eyebrows.

"Like the Shivers boys!" C. J. confirmed.

"Sounds great," Jenny scoffed sarcastically. "How are we supposed to get in there? You think they're going to hand over a castle to a bunch of kids so we can trap some criminals? Get serious!"

"As a matter of fact," C. J. replied patiently, "that's exactly what is going to happen.

"One of my Dad's best friends just happens to be in charge of the place," he went on.

"I used to go there when it was closed to the public and play hide and go seek with his kids, while he was working. It was great!"

"Okay," Jenny conceded. "So maybe we could get in there at night or something. Just us and the Shivers boys sneaking around in ninety-eight rooms of castle? Uh - uh. Count me out."

"Come on Jenny," C. J. chided her, "where's that Douglas spirit? At least we'll have the advantage of knowing our way around the place."

"I think it's a wonderful idea," Rolf chirped. "I think it's high time we went on the offensive."

"I'm in!" said Josh, thumping a fist into an open palm. "I guess..." he looked casually up at the sky, "if Jenny doesn't want to be part of the operation, we'll just have to go it alone."

"Yep," said C. J. shaking his head in mock sorrow. "It's too bad really."

"Yep," Rolf joined in. "It's a shame the girls will miss out, but I suppose there's nothing to be done."

"What do you mean, girls?" Cindy McKannin, who had been sitting quietly up to that point, suddenly blurted. "I want to be there."

Slowly four pairs of eyes turned to stare at Jenny. She shifted uneasily from one foot to another.

"All right," she finally relented, "I'll go along." She tossed her red hair defiantly. "I take it you have a plan?"

"I do," C. J. nodded.

At that moment Roy and Laura Douglas returned from their inspection of the motorhome.

"We found it," Roy reported. "The bug is under the dash by the heater. I'm no expert, but it looks powerful enough to pick up conversation from back in the motorhome."

"Good," C. J. grinned, "we wouldn't want them to miss what we have to say."

Roy and Laura surveyed the smiles on the five faces before them. "I've got a funny feeling you're up to something," Roy said slowly.

There was no answer but the grins became wider.

"You are up to something," Laura was frowning. "We better talk about it, whatever it is. This is a dangerous game these men are playing."

"We know that, Mom," Josh conceded. "We weren't going to do anything without letting you know."

He turned to C. J. "I think it's time we heard your plan."

At three o'clock the next afternoon, Laura Douglas and Jenny climbed into the cab of the motorhome. They had been selected to "set the bait," as C. J. referred to it.

After slamming the door and starting the engine for the sake of realism, Laura Douglas began the carefully rehearsed deceit.

"Now Jenny," she began, "you must be very careful not to let it slip to anyone where we've hidden Rolf."

"I'll be careful, Mom," Jenny replied carefully and distinctly, "but I still don't understand why we chose Casa Loma. Why a castle?"

"Your father and I think it's the last place Baron Steg and his men would look," Laura Douglas said, aiming her voice at the part of the dash that she knew held the concealed microphone.

"Well, one thing is for sure," Jenny continued, "the Shivers boys are too stupid to figure it out. When do we move the Prince up there?"

"Tonight," her mother answered. "When Casa Loma closes for the night, the Prince and C. J. will remain inside. There are parts of the castle that aren't used anymore so they'll be able to hide from the Casa Loma staff until everybody leaves."

"Isn't there a night watchman or anything?" Jenny asked.

"No," came the reply. "Just the caretaking staff and they go home about nine o'clock each night." Laura Douglas paused for emphasis, then added, "The two boys will have the whole castle to themselves after that."

"What about food?" Jenny pretended to show concern.

"Oh, they'll have backpacks with them with enough food for three days or so," Laura responded carefully.

"Prince Ludwig will be here soon and then we can get Rolf out of the castle and back with his father."

At that point, Laura gave her daughter a silent thumbs-up sign, then held her index finger to her lips. Jenny nodded and winked.

They sat for a few seconds in silence, the noise of

the idling motor the only sound the bug was picking up now.

"Well, here we are," Laura Douglas said, reaching down and shutting off the engine. "At McDonald's. Have you got that list of who wants what?"

"Sure have," Jenny lied with a grin. "Let's see . . . six Big Macs, eight fries, two quarter-pounders, (one with cheese), five chocolate shakes..."

As her voice droned the seemingly endless food order, Jenny and her mother stepped out of the motorhome, closed the doors and nearly doubled over with laughter. They scampered to the picnic tables, where the rest of the Douglas outfit were waiting for them.

For several seconds, neither of the two could talk, both having been overcome with giggles.

"Well, did you make it sound believable?" Roy Douglas was finally able to ask when Laura and Jenny had regained some of their composure.

"I . . . I . . . think . . . so," sputtered Laura Douglas, out of breath from laughing.

"Oh, you should have heard Mom," Jenny chuckled, "she could have won an Academy Award with her performance.

"You almost threw me off with that bit about McDonald's though," she laughed again.

"Well, your father told us he wanted realism," said Laura winking at her daughter.

"Oh, we gave 'em realism all right," Jenny asserted.

"But did you fool them?" Roy wondered aloud.

"If the Shivers boys were listening and if they are as stupid as we think they are . . . we fooled them," Laura announced confidently.

"There's no doubt about the stupid part," Jenny assured her. "I just hope they were listening."

"Well, we'll find out tonight," Roy Douglas told them. "I'm still not sure I'm doing the right thing letting this go ahead."

"Come on Dad," Josh reassured him, "we'll all be in the castle hidden away. If it looks like C. J. and Rolf are in any trouble, we'll be there to bail them out."

Roy Douglas shook his head, "Sometimes I can't believe the things I let you kids talk me into."

"Actually," Laura Douglas couldn't help laughing one more time, "this is getting to be kind of fun."

"C. J., you talked to your friend and we've got the place to ourselves?" Roy asked his nephew.

"Actually, Dad called him," C. J. replied. "He told him it was a special surprise we had planned for a famous visitor who we couldn't name at this time. Dad's friend didn't even question it. All he said was we'd have to pay for any damage we did."

"That's fair all right," Ben Bradley chipped in, "but what makes you so sure the Shivers boys will show up?"

"Ten thousand dollars," C. J. replied. "They want that money bad enough that they'll try anything to get at Rolf.

"All we're doing is making it a little easier for them,

that's all. And once we get them inside the castle . . ." His voice trailed off and a hint of a smile flickered at the corners of his mouth.

C. J. and Rolf had been sitting on a plush chesterfield in the middle of a huge room called the Great Hall.

It was located on the main floor of Casa Loma. The two boys had been there for over two hours. Behind them a large, very old grandfather clock had just chimed eleven times.

The Prince was sleepy. He yawned. "I would have thought they'd be here by now," he spoke in the hushed whisper he and C. J. had adopted since their arrival at the castle.

"Me too," C. J. nodded agreement.

"Do you think everybody's ready in the cellar?" Rolf whispered.

"They're ready," C. J. assured him. "That's the sixth time you've asked. I can guarantee you they're ready."

"Mmm," came Rolf's sleepy response.

The young Prince's head dropped to his chest. In another minute he was sound asleep.

C. J. forced himself to stay awake but as another half-hour went by with still no sign of the Shivers boys, he too fell asleep.

Suddenly, a loud noise jarred C. J. awake.

Had Miles Shivers not stumbled against a round

metal planter standing near the main entrance as he and Lefty crept through the unlocked front door, C. J. and Rolf would probably have been caught unawares.

Quickly C. J. shook Rolf to his senses, then pressed a finger to his lips. Rolf sat up sharply and was instantly aware of what was happening.

C. J. pointed in the direction of the front hall where the noise had come from. He and Rolf stood up without a sound and silently moved toward the place where they knew the Shivers boys had to be. The castle was in almost total darkness. Suddenly, the beam of a flashlight could be seen around the corner.

From this point on their timing had to be perfect. One mistake now and both C. J. and Rolf would be in grave danger.

They stopped in front of a staircase leading to the below-ground level of the castle. Around the corner and now only a few metres away, Lefty and Miles could be heard slowly coming closer. In another few seconds they would round the corner.

C. J. looked at his smaller companion. They could just see one another in the darkness.

C. J. silently mouthed the word "ready." Rolf nodded grimly.

The flashlight was at the corner. "Oh no, someone is here!" C. J. screamed at the top of his lungs. "Quick, Rolf, down the stairs! Run for the wine cellar!"

The two boys, their eyes well accustomed to the dark, scurried down the long, narrow staircase. They were careful not to go too quickly as they wanted the

Shivers brothers to be able to follow them.

As C. J. and the Prince reached the bottom of the stairs, they found themselves bathed in light as the glare of Lefty Shivers' flashlight beamed down from the top of the staircase.

They looked up and for a fraction of a second the four boys stared at one another without moving.

A triumphant grin spread over the evil features of Lefty Shivers. "We've got 'em!" he shouted for joy.

"Quick, in here!" C. J. grabbed Rolf's arm.

They disappeared through a massive oak door into the blackness of the castle's long-abandoned wine cellar. The rapid thudding of boots on stairs told them the Shivers boys were close behind them.

As they reached the bottom of the staircase, Lefty and Miles didn't hesitate, but plunged quickly into the long, sinister cellar.

Once inside the low-ceilinged wine cellar, the two pursuers stopped to get their bearings. As they did, the huge, heavy door crashed shut behind them.

The would-be kidnappers spun around and stared dumbfounded at the closed door.

"What happened?" Miles shouted, terror rising in his voice.

"Never mind that," Lefty growled, "those two kids are in here somewhere. Now let's find them."

Lefty, with his younger brother close to his side, shone the light on the long, bare wine racks that rimmed the spooky room.

From one end to the other, the two pursuers combed the wine cellar. At the far end, only a bare wall stared back at them.

"Where could they have got to?" Lefty spun desperately one way, then the other.

"Maybe they didn't come in here," Miles offered lamely.

"We saw them come in here," Lefty snarled at his brother. "We'll search this castle from one end to the other if we have to, but we're gonna find 'em."

He stepped up to the door that had mysteriously closed behind them, turned the handle and pressed his shoulder to the cold, wooden surface.

It didn't budge.

He tried again with the same result. "Come here," he beckoned furiously at his younger brother, "help me."

Together they pressed against the door with every ounce of their strength. The massive slab remained immovable.

Lefty raced to the far end of the cellar and back again, looking for another entrance, a window, any way out of this frightening, silent prison.

And slowly he realized that there *was* no way out. Somehow . . . he didn't know how; he and his brother had been tricked. And now, as a result of that trick, he and Miles were trapped inside a wine cellar.

He had to think.

Yet, the more he thought, the more he came to the grim realization that two of the people he hated most in the world had outwitted him again.

Behind him, he could hear Miles sniffling. This couldn't be happening to them.

Lefty's fury mounted. Suddenly he leaped up like a man gone mad and smashed his fist against the unfeeling door.

Stony, unyielding silence answered his tantrum. Beaten, Lefty slumped down the wall and sat on the floor. Across from him, Miles looked at him through tear-filled eyes.

The captors were caught!

Chapter Seventeen

At about the same time that the Shivers boys were coming to the realization that they were trapped in the wine cellar, a very different scene was taking place in another part of the castle.

In the ornate room that had once been the study of the original owner of Casa Loma, Sir Henry Pellatt, a rather merry celebration was taking place.

C. J., Rolf, Josh, Jenny, Cindy and Roy and Laura Douglas were boisterously congratulating each other at having put one over on the Shivers boys.

C. J.'s Dad, Bill Findlay, was there too. He had been asked by C. J. to be a part of the plan to trap Miles and Lefty and had been only too willing to get involved.

In fact, it was he and Roy Douglas who had been hiding behind the oak door that led into the wine cellar and had slammed it shut after the Shivers boys had gone inside.

Josh and the three female members of the plan had been hiding in another part of the castle, poised to escape and go for help if C. J.'s plan had backfired.

"Okay, okay," said Roy Douglas signalling for quiet. "Now I know that there is one question that we all want answered. How *did* you two get out of that wine cellar?"

All eyes turned in the direction of C. J. and Rolf. Up to that point C. J. had told them only what their individual roles were in the plan, but had let no one in on how he and Rolf were to execute their dramatic disappearing act.

"Well, that's why I asked you all to come into this room," said C. J. assuming his best Sherlock Holmes' pose.

"Please observe carefully." He crossed to the wall farthest from the entrance. "Do you see anything unusual?"

No one did.

Turning to the group with a flourish he said, "Note ... nothing up the sleeves..."

"Will you cut it out," Jenny interrupted him, "and tell us how you got out of that wine cellar."

"Of course, of course, all in good time, my dear." C. J. was enjoying himself.

"Oh brother," Jenny groaned.

"Patience, dear," Laura laughed, "I'm sure he'll tell us eventually."

"It's elementary, you see," C. J. began again. "Watch closely." With that he turned and pressed a panel in the wall. Incredibly, a door swung creating a space in what had looked like a solid wall.

"Well, I'll be doggoned," Roy Douglas said shaking his head in disbelief.

"A secret door!" Cindy gasped.

"Awesome!" Jenny breathed.

"How did you know about that?" Josh asked his cousin.

"It's like I said," C. J. crossed his arms smugly, "this was a great place to play hide and go seek. But I haven't completed my explanation," he continued. "Come closer, my friends."

They pressed toward the opening and looked inside. "You see, of course, a staircase leading down." C. J. strutted around the room as he spoke.

Only C. J.'s father and Rolf hadn't bothered to come forward and look at the secret passage. Both of them already knew about it.

"It leads down to... " Rolf began.

"Uh-uh-uh," C. J. stopped him in mid-sentence. "Please try to control yourself young man."

Under his breath he whispered at the Prince, "I want to tell them." He went on. "It leads down to the wine cellar ... and in the northwest wall of the cellar is a secret door just like this one." C. J. grinned triumphantly at his appreciative audience.

"That's fantastic," Josh breathed.

"Wait a minute," Jenny spun quickly around. "You mean the Shivers boys are just at the bottom on those steps?"

She backed away from the secret passage.

"At the bottom of those steps and behind a wall that looks just like any other wall," C. J. acknowledged.

"They couldn't find the panel that opens the door in a million years. In fact," he continued, "the only part of this whole operation that really had me worried was finding the panel in the dark. And I know where it is."

"Yes," Rolf agreed readily, "if that secret door down there hadn't opened the first time, we would have been in deep trouble."

"You're sure they can't get out?" Jenny didn't sound convinced.

"It's all right, Jen," Bill Findlay reassured her. "They can't hear us and they can't get out."

"Well," Josh wondered aloud, "what now? Do we just leave 'em there?"

"Nope," C. J. answered, "the plan isn't completed yet. That's where Dad comes in."

"I'll be making a couple of phone calls as soon as we leave here," Mr. Findlay explained. "One will be an anonymous call to the police. In an hour or so a police car will arrive to investigate a report of prowlers at Casa Loma. Our friends in the wine cellar will undoubtedly be arrested.

"And there won't be any connection with the Prince so there needn't be any bad publicity for Mendenstein. I'm sure Lefty and Miles aren't going to tell the police that the reason they are in Casa Loma at midnight is so they can kidnap the Crown Prince of a foreign state."

"But what's to keep them from getting Baron Steg to just come down and bail them out first thing in the morning?" Laura Douglas asked.

"Ah, now that's where the second phone call comes in," Mr. Findlay said with a smile. "I've already arranged for a photographer from *The Toronto Globe and Mail* to be here. The phone call will just be to let them know when. As the police lead our two friends out of the wine cellar, the newspaper photographer will be sure to get a nice picture for tomorrow's paper."

"Hey, I get it!" Roy Douglas interjected. "If there's one thing Baron Steg won't be happy about, it's having his boys' faces plastered all over the paper."

"Right," Mr. Findlay agreed. "In fact, my guess is, if they're smart, these two characters will stay in jail where they'll be safe until this is all over and Baron Steg and his men are out of town."

"And if they do get out of jail," C. J. put in, "I'll bet they hightail it for Alberta as fast as they can go."

"You know, cousin," Jenny said pursing her lips thoughtfully, "I have to hand it to you ... this was a pretty good plan."

"Pretty good?" C. J. exclaimed in mock anguish.

"Okay, really good!" Jenny corrected herself. "I think we're finally rid of the Shivers boys."

"But, we're not out of the woods yet," Josh reminded her, "not until we have Rolf and his father back together."

"I've been thinking about that too," Roy Douglas said rubbing a big hand over his jaw. "I have a theory I want to try out on the rest of you.

"I really doubt that Baron Steg and his men will try

to kidnap the Prince again. Especially now that the Shivers boys are out of the picture."

Rolf shook his head stubbornly when he said, "Mr. Douglas, you are wrong if you think these men will give up. They will not."

"I'm not suggesting they'll give up, Rolf," Roy concurred. "I think they just might change their strategy, that's all."

"What do you mean, Dad?" Josh asked.

"They don't *need* to kidnap Rolf," Roy explained. "All they have to do is make it impossible for us to get the Prince back to his father."

Addressing himself to Rolf, Roy said, "Baron Steg has undoubtedly been sending word from time to time to your father that everything is going well on your tour of Canada. If we aren't able to get you through to him, Steg will make up some story about an accident. Then once your father has left the country believing some terrible accident has claimed his son, the Baron and his men will have all the time in the world to... finish the job."

No one asked for an explanation of what Roy had meant with his final ominous words.

"So you figure they'll just follow us around and if we make a move toward Prince Ludwig when he gets here ... they'll move in!" Bill Findlay said as he paced back and forth in the study.

"Or," Roy Douglas surmised, "they might just watch Prince Ludwig. It might be easier for them to stay between him and us that way."

"Boy, that's going to make it tough all right," Josh murmured.

"Especially since we don't know if everyone in the Prince's own entourage can be trusted," Roy Douglas pointed out.

"So what do we do, Dad?" Jenny asked.

"Well, I'm sure there's no way we'll be able to just march into the hotel and get to the Prince," her father noted. "That'd be the easiest place for them to watch.

"Rolf, do you know what public appearances your father has planned during his visit?" Roy asked."

The prince thought hard. "No, I really don't know what is on his itinerary. I know he is only going to be here for two days," Rolf told them.

"We've got to think of a way to break through the ring of security that will be around Prince Ludwig," Roy said. "Between the normal security for visiting heads of state and Baron Steg's boys watching out for us, it won't be... "

"Hold on," Rolf snapped his fingers, "Father is supposed to play in a polo match the day before he leaves."

"Ah, now that has possibilities." Roy's eyes narrowed as he studied the young Prince. "Do you know where the match is going to be played?"

Not really," Rolf answered shaking his head, "other than I remember him saying it was in a big park."

"Hmm," Roy thought out loud. "A big park, eh!"

"High Park!" C. J. exclaimed. "It must be High Park. It's a huge place."

"And they certainly could play polo there," Bill Findlay added. "In fact the park is patrolled by policemen on horseback, so horses are right at home in High Park. I'll bet C. J.'s right."

"The day before he leaves," Roy mused... "That means the match is being played next Saturday, on the day after the rodeo ends. I think we'd better plan to make our move there. But it won't be easy. I'm certain Baron Steg will do everything he can to stop us."

"High Park it is then," Josh set his chin grimly. "That's where Rolf will get back together with his father."

"Right," Jenny and Cindy chorused confidently.

"Saturday's the day," C. J. added, determination written on his face.

"Now," Roy Douglas reminded them soberly, "all we have to do is figure out how we're going to do it."

Chapter Eighteen

That fateful Saturday seemed to approach at breakneck speed.

The morning after "The Casa Loma Caper," as it had been designated by C. J., the front page of *The Toronto Globe and Mail* had been decorated by the menacing faces of Lefty and Miles Shivers.

And as had been predicted, there hadn't been a peep out of the two hoodlums since. A couple of discreet inquiries by Mr. Findlay brought the news that Lefty had declined to post bail and had requested that he and his brother be allowed to remain in custody until the following week. With that out of the way, the Douglas Rodeo outfit had focused its collective attention on the rodeo at Maple Leaf Gardens. It wound up being a smash success.

Huge crowds had greeted the competing cowboys every night and cheered from start to finish. The stock had been outstanding, showing no ill-effects of the long trip east.

For Josh, Jenny, C. J. and Cindy the results had not been what they had hoped for, but their lack of personal success was offset by the thrill of competing in the Gardens.

Of the four, C. J. had been closest to placing, but came up a couple of points short on a mediocre steer.

Nevertheless, the crowd had responded to the performance of their hometown hero as if he'd made a ninety-eight point ride.

At the beginning of each performance, Roy Douglas had designated C. J. to circle the arena with the Canadian flag during the national anthem. It was a breathtaking sight as the Toronto teenager mounted on his spectacular black horse slowly moved around the arena floor. The entire building was in darkness but for the spotlight that was trained on C. J. and Doc Holliday.

For C. J. it had been a very special homecoming and there were plenty of moist eyes each evening during the singing of *O Canada*.

The rodeo's final performance had been Friday night. It had been sold out and the capacity crowd had given the rodeo a send-off that was guaranteed to bring the cowboys and cowgirls back the next year.

But now the moment had come. Saturday morning had dawned on a warm, cloudless day. Not a breath of wind was in the air.

Everyone connected with the Douglas Rodeo outfit was preparing for the final countdown to the attempt to reunite the Princes.

Josh and Jenny had worked into the early morning hours each night after the rodeo putting together a plan.

Roy Douglas had refined it and C. J., because of his familiarity with the area, had diagrammed it. The plan was simple enough. A small band of riders was to ride on horseback from the C.N.E. grounds down a parkway along the beach that bordered Lake Ontario.

At Lakeshore Boulevard the riders were to turn north, go under the freeway overpass and arrive at the southeast corner of High Park. At that point the band of riders with Prince Rolf in the middle would begin a life-and-death ride at breakneck speed through the park. Their instructions were simple. They were not to stop for anything or anyone until they were alongside Prince Ludwig on the polo field.

There were two problems. One was that High Park had been left in a natural state with some areas that were heavily wooded. The riders would have to be careful not to be separated from one another during their high-speed ride.

The other difficulty was that although they were certain Baron Steg and his men would be ready for them, no one was sure what kind of defence the evil Baron would throw around Prince Ludwig to keep them out.

Roy Douglas had cautioned everyone that it was not outside the realm of possibility that they would be shot at. He told them in no uncertain terms that if they felt that their lives were in danger, they were to retreat to safety as quickly as possible.

It had been decided that for practical purposes the mounted contingent would consist of C. J. in the lead, Josh at the back and Cindy and Jenny at the sides.

The Prince, of course, was to be in the middle, protected on all sides as much as possible from whatever it was they were about to run into.

The adults were to circle the park in CB radio-equipped vehicles, trying to spot Baron Steg and his men. Roy and Laura Douglas would be in one vehicle, Ben Bradley in another and Len Tucker in a third.

A fourth vehicle, manned by Clayton's mother and father, was to be stationed at the southeast corner of High Park. It, too, was equipped with a CB radio.

If the scouts in any of the other three vehicles should spot something that indicated that the riders had no chance of succeeding, Mr. and Mrs. Findlay would be able to stop them before they entered the park and the mission would be aborted.

The usually light atmosphere that accompanied any activity involving the Douglas ranch crew was absent as the horses were being prepared.

The five young riders were especially silent, all lost in their own thoughts. The only sounds heard were the creaking of leather and the occasional slap of a latigo strap against a saddle.

Even the horses seemed to sense that something about the impending ride was different.

Doc Holliday pranced up and down the whole time he was being saddled. Jenny's mare, Sugar, snorted and whinnied. Cindy's barrel racing horse – a grey gelding called Catfish – pawed the pavement impatiently, first with one foot, then the other.

It was decided that Rolf would ride Doc Holliday. Although the stallion was a one-man horse and that man was C. J., Roy Douglas felt that if something went wrong during the ride, it would be important that the Prince be mounted on the fastest, strongest horse. That horse was unquestionably Doc Holliday. The fact that C. J. would be close at hand should keep the big stallion calm.

C. J. and Josh would be riding the pickup horses – C. J. on the paint horse he'd been riding during the wild morning adventure at the Calgary Stampede and Josh on Ben Bradley's other pickup horse, a tall, good-looking buckskin. Although it was the buckskin that had fled in panic that fateful Stampede morning, the horse was powerful and "could run a hole in the wind," as Ben Bradley put it.

They were ready. The five riders were scheduled

to leave at the same time as those in vehicles. That way, by the time the riders reached the park, the scouts would have had time to circle the park a few times.

It was time to ride!

Chapter Nineteen

As soon as they were mounted up, the four older riders turned their attention protectively to the Prince.

"Saddle feel o.k.?" Josh asked.

"Cinch tight enough?" Jenny questioned.

"How are your stirrups ... they feel long enough?" C. J. wanted to know.

"Everything's fine," Rolf assured them, his mouth set grimly. "I'm ready when you are."

Luckily, Rolf was an experienced rider from his school days in England. Not so lucky was the fact that all of the riding he had done was English riding in the flat saddle that was part of that style.

The last three days had been spent in intensive western riding lessons under the supervision of Roy Douglas. Roy was confident that the Prince would be able to handle both the ride and the powerful stallion beneath him.

"Good luck!" Laura Douglas called as the five riders turned and slowly made their way towards the C.N.E. grounds exit.

"This is a good omen," C. J. announced as they passed through a magnificent set of gates that served as both entrance and exit for Exhibition Place, site of the C.N.E. grounds.

"Why's that?" Jenny asked him.

"These are called the Princes' Gates. They're named to honor two Princes. And now, here we are, starting out from the Princes' Gates to reunite two Princes."

"Did *you* make that up?" Jenny asked skeptically.

"Honest," C. J. crossed his heart, "that's what they're called."

The little band of riders lapsed again into silence as they waited at the traffic lights leading onto Lakeshore Boulevard.

They drew plenty of stares as they crossed on the

green light. All five were garbed in cowboy hats, neckerchiefs, and chaps. Passing motorists stared at the unusual posse crossing one of the busiest thoroughfares in Toronto.

Once across the road, the riders passed through a small park and arrived at the Martin Goodman Trail, a long, winding pathway running adjacent to Lake Ontario.

C. J. had estimated it would take about an hour to reach High Park. Much of that time would be spent on this pathway which was actually designed for joggers, walkers and cyclists.

For a quarter of an hour they rode in grim silence, never once acknowledging the cheerful banter of passers-by.

Cindy decided to try to ease the tension. "C. J., I'm surprised you haven't given our expedition a name," she said.

"After all, wasn't it *you* who brought us 'The Casa Loma Caper', and what was the one at the Calgary Stampede ... 'The Great Tunnel Undertaking'?"

"Yuk!" Jenny responded. "Tunnel *Under*taking. What a terrible pun."

"Actually I didn't think it was too bad," C. J. laughed. "And, by the way I do have a name for this. I call it 'The Ride for the Crown.'"

"That's not bad," Josh acknowledged.

"Sure beats The Great Tunnel Undertaking," Jenny snorted.

"What do *you* think, Rolf?" Cindy asked.

The Prince was looking distractedly around. He obviously hadn't been paying attention.

"What ... oh, uh ... yes ... that's good ... Ride for the Crown ... It certainly will be that, all right," he stammered. "At least ... I hope so."

The others exchanged looks. It was obvious Rolf was, if not actually afraid, at least very nervous.

"You ever play *I spy with my little eye*?" Josh asked, as if they were merely out for a quiet afternoon ride in the country.

"No, I guess I haven't," the Prince replied.

"Well, it's time you learned," Jenny announced.

For the better part of an hour the little band of riders clip-clopped their way over the paved pathway and engaged in a rousing game of *I Spy*.

It was the perfect diversion. By the time they reached the point where they had to turn north and leave the pathway, they had identified most of Toronto's major landmarks and everything that was moving on Lake Ontario.

Even Jenny's often maligned hair had been one of the *I Spy* targets.

The game had done what it was designed to do: it had taken Rolf's mind off what was waiting for them at High Park.

"Okay, gang, this is where we leave the trail and join up with High Park," C. J. announced. "We go over Lakeshore Boulevard, then under the Gardiner Expressway and the Queensway. We'll come out at Parkside Drive right at the corner of High Park.

"Mom and Dad will be at that corner," he reminded them. "If there are any messages they need to get to us, Mom will be outside the car. If they're both in the car, we keep going."

"Okay, let's get off the horses for a minute and everyone check their cinches one last time," Josh ordered.

As everyone complied with the directive, C. J. repeated for the fortieth time what was to happen when they would reach the park.

"We start out at the trot. Remember this park is 400 acres and the polo match is on the other side of Grenadier Pond on the west side and almost to the north end of the park," he said.

"We start to lope once we come out of that first ravine. From then on, there's no turning back and we just keep going until we see the polo game. That's all there is to it," he concluded with a half-hearted attempt at a grin.

"It's sure going to ruin the game," Jenny chuckled.

"I'm sure my Father will forgive us," said Rolf. He, too, was trying to appear lighthearted.

"Okay, let's mount up," Josh said quietly. "It's time to ride."

Back in the saddles, they moved quickly across the concrete tentacles that twisted their way by the lake's northern edge.

It took only a few minutes to cover the territory between the trail they had been on and the edge of High Park.

They paused as they reached the park and looked sharply around. There was nothing to indicate that this would be any different from any other day at any other park.

C. J. spotted his father's dark blue Oldsmobile parked on the other side of Parkside Drive. Both his father and mother were sitting in the car staring straight ahead.

"We go," C. J. said, his voice barely above a whisper.

They quickly formed the pattern they would use for the entire ride, with Rolf in the middle. The five riders urged their horses into a brisk trot.

Chapter Twenty

The horses were glad for the opportunity to stretch out and pick up the pace. C. J., in the lead, rode grimly, looking uneasily from side to side for signs of the Baron or his men.

As the five riders passed by a parking lot on the left, each pair of eyes scanned the lot for the pickup truck that had been seen at the CNE grounds.

All five breathed sighs of relief when they saw no sign of the vehicle. As the horses settled into the comfortable jog-trot that was excellent for covering a lot of ground in a short time, the riders allowed themselves to relax a little and enjoy the ride through the picturesque park.

They passed a couple of small ponds, a cook shelter and a children's playground. Near the playground, several children and their parents were feeding ducks and geese in another pond.

"I wish we could be spending the day having a picnic and feeding the birds," Cindy said only half-jokingly.

Rolf nodded in soundless agreement. As the riders passed the playground, some of the children waved and called out happily to them.

Josh returned the greeting with a solemn tip of his cowboy hat and Jenny made a failed attempt at a smile. The other three rode on, oblivious to the stares and shouts of the park visitors.

"I wonder what they'd think if they knew why we were riding through this park," C. J. pondered aloud.

No one answered him. The circle of riders crossed the first of a series of roads they were to encounter, then found themselves surrounded by huge trees.

"These are red oak," C. J. explained, as they passed beneath the stately towers. "The trees up ahead are black oak."

"Geez," Jenny groaned, "even at a time like this he's doing his tour-guide thing again."

"This is where we turn west," C. J. instructed and stuck his tongue out at his cousin.

They swung their horses to the left, crossed a pathway for a trackless train, and arrived at a grove of white pines. Quickly the riders moved through the trees, across a stretch of open ground and suddenly came upon a wide, densely bushed ravine. So far, everything had been exactly as C. J. and his countless maps had said it would be. Better yet was the fact that they had not seen any sign of trouble.

The ravine was a concern because it would provide plenty of opportunity for their pursuers to stay out of sight.

If the Baron was planning an ambush, there was no better place to stage one than in this forest within a park. Each of the riders was thinking just that as they pulled to a halt at the edge of the ravine.

"So far, so good." Jenny breathed.

"You don't suppose we were wrong and they might just let us ride right up to the polo match, do you?" Cindy speculated hopefully.

"Don't count on it," Josh told her.

"Let's get going," C. J. said, starting his horse down the steep embankment of the ravine. The rest of the horses followed, sliding and groping their way to the bottom.

Picking their way through the underbrush and sassafras, horse chestnut, pine and buckthorn trees that seemed to fill every square inch of the ravine was a long, slow process. Their biggest concern was becoming separated from one another and while they would have preferred to ride in silence in case Baron Steg's men were nearby, they decided it would be best to keep talking to one another to ensure that no one became lost.

"Nice scenery, eh?" Jenny offered.

"I guess so if you're into bush," Josh replied.

C. J. feigned anger when he said, "Hey guys, this is typical Ontario plant life; show a little respect will you."

"What do you think, Rolf?" Cindy called.

"Lovely ... I guess," came the sober reply.

And so the conversation continued as they slowly walked their way through the seemingly endless ravine.

At last they emerged from the heavy growth and scrambled up the far embankment. The two girls heaved sighs of relief as they emerged from the ravine.

"I'm glad that's over with," Rolf stated in a shaky voice.

"All right, we're about half-way there," C. J. announced, "but the toughest part is still ahead of us. We'll be in the open from here on. Everybody ready?"

The horses seemed to sense that the real drama was about to unfold and pranced about, impatient to be underway.

The five riders reset their formation with Prince Rolf once again in the middle of the other four.

"Let's go!" C. J. cried and they were off at a gallop.

They charged past a huge botanical garden on the right, but none of them was in any mood to notice. Each was intent on the ride and the danger that might be lying ahead.

The power of the horses carried them swiftly across an expanse of open ground. They quickly passed a service road that appeared to lead in the direction of the botanical gardens.

The four teenage riders took turns glancing at Rolf to see how the Prince was making out aboard Doc Holliday. The last thing any of them wanted at this point was a runaway. But the Prince seemed perfectly in control although the great black stallion was obviously enjoying the furious pace they were maintaining as they raced through the park.

At the front of the band of riders, C. J. suddenly called out, "Pull up," and began to rein in his own horse. The others followed suit and in a moment all five were gingerly stepping across a paved road.

As they reached the other side, C. J. turned in the saddle, "Well, we're almost there; everybody all right?"

None of them had a chance to answer as suddenly Jenny pointed to her left and shrieked, "Look!"

Every eye turned in the direction she was pointing. There they were!

Roaring down the road toward the riders was the dreaded pickup truck. Even more frightening was the sight of several men on horseback emerging from a stand of birch trees and mulberry bushes.

Instinctively, C. J. looked to his right and gave an involuntary shudder as he saw a second group of riders coming from that direction. They were still a long way off but closing ground fast.

There was no question of turning back. The only hope was to go straight ahead and try to beat the deadly vice that was closing in on them.

"Come on!" C. J. urged.

Desperately, they dug heels into their mounts and instantaneously the willing horses were charging after C. J. on the paint.

Even at the breakneck speed they were travelling, the four older riders were able to manoeuvre their horses so as to keep Rolf in the relative safety of the centre of their little formation.

The Baron's men were clearly on well-conditioned, fast horses and they were gaining ground in a hurry, travelling at an angle that would almost surely allow them to head off the five fleeing riders.

Gamely the little band bent lower in their saddles and urged their horses on. It was clear that the danger would not come from the front but from the sides.

C. J. angled his horse to the left to try to maintain a guard with Cindy on that side. Josh moved up and joined Jenny on the Prince's right. It was their only alternative although all of them knew that it would be almost impossible to hold off the numbers of riders that were fast closing in on them.

At the front of the group charging in from the left was a swarthy, bearded man on a big, athletic bay horse. The evil-looking man was bearing down hard on the Prince and his badly outnumbered escort. His eyes never left the Prince.

C. J. could see the dark-faced attacker would be alongside Rolf in a matter of seconds. He had to do *something*.

At the last possible second, C. J. swerved his own horse and in perfect pickup man fashion headed off the charging leader of Baron Steg's men.

C. J. drove the powerful shoulder of the paint hard into the side of the intruder's big bay.

The bay stumbled, righted itself and stopped in its tracks, all the steam taken out of it by the hard blow it had taken.

The paint barely broke stride and was quickly back up to full speed. C. J. looked behind him and allowed himself the luxury of a grin as he saw that two more of the attackers, unable to stop quickly enough, had run into the first man and his suddenly motionless horse.

One man was on the ground trying desperately to hold onto the reins of his frantic horse, while the first man was cursing loudly. C. J. wasn't sure whether the man was cursing his startled horse, the men who had run into him or whether the vile language was being directed at C. J. himself, but at any rate there wasn't time to ponder the question.

To the Prince's right the action was getting heavy. There, a huge man, wearing a long black rainslicker, had pulled ahead of the other pursuing riders and was zeroing in on the Prince.

Josh, having witnessed the success of C. J.'s manoeuvre, tried the same thing on his side.

Unfortunately, the man in black was a better rider than the other attacker and deftly checked his horse for a split second, forcing Josh on the buckskin to miss.

Josh looked over his shoulder and saw the powerful-looking man alongside the Prince trying to pull Rolf off his horse with a massive free arm.

Quickly Josh changed directions again and pulled alongside the hulking attacker. The problem would be stopping this man who probably weighed twice as much as he did.

There was no choice. Josh jumped from his own horse onto the back of the big man. He got his arms around the attacker's neck and hung on for dear life.

The man's bulk was working against him. Brought

back in the saddle by Josh's death grip on his throat, the big man pulled back instinctively on the reins. His horse stopped sharply, then reared up high.

As the horse went up, Josh and the attacker fell hard to the ground, with Josh on top. The big man landed hard on his back, and the air rushed from his lungs with a loud whoosh.

The attacker was unable to move and Josh took advantage of the opportunity to regain his feet and run to the buckskin. The horse had stopped not far from where Josh and the now stunned assailant had landed.

Josh jumped quickly into the saddle and was about to race after the rest of the riders who were now some distance ahead, when the reins were suddenly pulled out of his hands.

Josh looked around and there beside him was the grim, unsmiling face of Baron Steg. In his hand was a gun. It was aimed directly at Josh's chest.

"You will not attempt to move or escape, please, or I will not hesitate to shoot you." The Baron's heavily accented voice was cold and deadly when he spoke these words..

Josh knew that he meant what he said. He was forced to sit and watch what was taking place up ahead.

"I have given orders for them to shoot," the Baron explained with icy venom dripping from his voice. "It will all be over in a few moments. You may watch."

The Baron's mouth curled into a cruel smile.

The rest of the riders were hurtling across the park, now just a few hundred metres from the polo field which was hidden behind more trees.

C. J. had moved right alongside Rolf with the two girls directly behind them.

There was no more thought of riding in formation. They were thinking of only one thing – escape – and that meant riding faster and harder than any of them had ever done before.

Another rider came into view from the corner of C. J.'s eyes. C. J. looked over and his look of grim determination swiftly changed to one of horror.

The man was brandishing a gun and that gun was aimed at C. J. and the Prince. Behind the gunman, cries of "Shoot, shoot," were coming from his companions.

The man with the gun swung his horse closer as if to eliminate any chance of missing. There were now just a few metres separating the hunter and his helpless prey.

Then, from out of nowhere, accompanied by a blood-curdling yell, came the blurred images of another rider, of a hand raised and of that hand bringing down a club on the arm of the surprised attacker.

The man with the gun yelled in pain as the gun dropped harmlessly to the ground.

Only then was C. J. able to determine that the person who had saved them was... Jenny and the club was a tree branch. Drawing abreast of C. J. and Rolf, she threw back her head and repeated the wild yell. Then she turned toward C. J. and the Prince and grinned the oddest grin either of them had ever seen.

The fleeing riders were now riding four abreast. They knew they had to keep going even though they realized Josh was back in the midst of their pursuers. They were hoping that Baron Steg and his men only wanted the Prince and would be content with having Josh out of the way for the moment.

The horses were tiring. They had probably ridden twice as far as those of the Baron's men and were noticeably slowing.

Suddenly, there was a popping sound behind them and a bullet whistled just over their heads. Then came another! And another!

It was as if things began to happen in slow motion. Without warning and without a sound, Doc Holliday went down. The Prince flew over the stallion's head and hit the ground rolling. He must have rolled ten times before coming to a stop.

C. J. pulled hard on the paint and got him stopped alongside Rolf.

"Come on!" C. J. screamed at the fallen Prince. "Get up here with me."

"I... I... can't," the Prince gasped, "my... leg... I can't."

"Keep going!" C. J. hollered at Cindy and Jenny, who had managed to stop their horses and were coming back. "Keep going. Get help!"

It was too late. They were all quickly surrounded by the Baron's men. Two of the attackers dismounted and grabbed the injured Prince under each arm. Rolf cried out in pain as he was wrenched to his feet.

Tears of rage blinded C. J. They had almost made it. They had been so close.

Then, strangely, the popping sound started again. Only this time it was coming from the opposite direction.

Suddenly the two men holding the Prince unceremoniously dropped him and scrambled madly for their horses.

At the same time, C. J. became aware of a series of whoops and shrieks coming from the direction of Jenny and Cindy. As he turned to look, he saw the strangest and, at the same time, most welcome sight he had ever witnessed. Racing toward them at the dead gallop was a bizarre array of policemen, polo players and cowboys.

"Awright!" C. J. shouted to Rolf who had struggled to his feet, "it's the cavalry!"

"What odd-looking cavalry you have here," Rolf calmly noted.

He was, in fact, quite correct in his observation.

At the head of the group of rescuers were Roy Douglas and Ben Bradley, both looking terribly uncomfortable in polo-style saddles. Behind them were several of Toronto's mounted policemen, guns drawn and firing into the air. Interspersed among the policemen and cowboys were the polo players, waving their polo mallets like war clubs.

C. J. was vaguely aware of movement around him as Baron Steg's men frantically tried to escape.

Jumping down from his horse, C. J. threw his arms around Rolf. "We did it!" he shouted.

The Prince had recovered from his fall. He threw back his head and allowed himself a mighty "Yahoo!"

As the two men who had tried to grab the Prince hurried away, C. J. called cheerfully to them. "Hey, guys, stick around, we're all gonna head over and feed the ducks and geese after a while!"

"And you won't want to miss the wiener roast later!" Rolf's high-pitched voice sang out gleefully.

One of the polo players pulled his horse up alongside the two boys and climbed down.

"Father!" cried Rolf. The two of them embraced joyfully.

Roy Douglas and Ben Bradley joined the group just as Josh rode up from behind.

For a moment no one spoke much as relieved hugs were being exchanged all around.

Josh broke the silence. "I figured we'd had it," he observed. "I didn't think you'd be able to come and help us."

"We found a sympathetic policeman who spoke to a couple of Prince Ludwig's security men and the next thing we knew we had a posse organized," Roy Douglas replied.

"I'll tell you one thing ... I'm awful glad to get out of that saddle," Ben Bradley added with a grimace as he climbed down from his horse. The comment and the look of agony on the big cowboy's face brought a shout of laughter.

As the laughter subsided, Rolf said softly, "You can't imagine what these people have done for me, Father! They risked their lives... they..." The young Prince stopped, as a lump formed in his throat making it difficult for him to speak.

"I think I understand perfectly, son," the deep, pleasant voice of the reigning Prince of Mendenstein responded. Together the Royal pair turned to look at the cluster of cowboys and cowgirls gathered around them.

The eyes of both the Prince and Crown Prince shone with unspoken gratitude and for a long time no one said anything.

"Geez!" C. J. exclaimed suddenly. "What about Doc? He went down hard. I thought he was shot. Where is he? Is he okay?" The words came in a torrent.

"It's okay, C. J.," Cindy said softly. "He must have just stumbled. He got right up. Jenny and I caught him and he's over there enjoying some of High Park's lawn right now."

Sure enough the sweat-soaked stallion was contentedly nibbling blades of grass as if nothing of importance had taken place at all.

"Hey, there's one more thing I'd like to know." C. J. addressed his beaming cousin, "Where did you get that branch you used on the guy with the gun?"

"Oh that," Jenny replied with a grin, "I grabbed it as we were going through the ravine; I thought it might come in handy.

"By the way," she added, "what did you think of my war cry?"

With that, High Park in the middle of Toronto, Ontario, Canada echoed once more with the sound of Jenny's blood-curdling yell. Instantly there were several more versions of the eerie sound as everyone in the group tried to duplicate the raucous noise.

When the racket and laughter finally died down, Roy Douglas said to Prince Ludwig, "I'm sorry Your Highness, but it looks like we've ruined your polo match."

"That's quite all right," the Prince replied with a wink. "Your Canadian team was beating us rather badly. But I think I won the biggest prize of all today," he added with his arm around Rolf's shoulders.

Epilogue

The spotlight found C. J. Findlay in the middle of the arena. The crowd fell silent. The boy spoke in a clear, resonant voice.

"Heavenly Father, we pause, mindful of the many blessings You have bestowed upon us at this rodeo and we pray that You will be with us in the arena of life. We don't ask for special favors. We don't ask to draw around a chute-fighting horse or to never break a barrier. Nor do we ask for all daylight runs or not to draw the steer that won't lay. Help us Lord, to live our lives in such a manner that when we make up that last inevitable ride to the country up there where the grass grows lush, green and stirrup-high and the water runs cool, clear and deep that You, as our last Judge, will tell us our entry fees are paid. Amen."

As C. J. finished the recitation of the Cowboy Prayer, the spotlight switched to Ben Bradley, and the pickup man began singing the Canadian national anthem.

He sang the words in a rich, mellow baritone voice that always surprised people hearing the raw-boned, rough-edged cowboy for the first time.

As the anthem was concluded, the crowd in

Edmonton's Northlands Coliseum sat back in anticipation of what was to come.

The final performance of the Canadian Finals Rodeo was about to begin. The Boys' Steer Riding was scheduled to be the third event on the program. For the six contestants there wasn't much time to get ready. C. J. and Josh hurried to the area behind the chutes and fell to work resining their ropes and preparing themselves mentally for their upcoming rides.

The voice of Hank Parker boomed over the microphone. "Ladies and Gentlemen, before our rodeo gets underway tonight, we have two very special guests with us this evening. This will come as a complete surprise to almost everyone here. As we lower a microphone into the middle of the arena, I'd ask that you give a very special Canadian welcome to the Prince and Crown Prince of Mendenstein – Prince Ludwig and his son Crown Prince Rolf."

C. J. and Josh were dumbfounded. They dropped their ropes and ran to the chutes. They climbed up just in time to see the two Princes making their way into the centre of the arena. They hadn't seen Rolf or his father since the royal pair had departed Toronto the day after the thrilling ride through High Park.

Now here it was, almost four months later, and they were here ... at the Canadian Finals.

Prince Ludwig stepped to the microphone. He spoke with a distinct but pleasant German accent. "My Canadian friends," he began. "As most of you know, my son and I – indeed everyone in the

Principality we come from – owes a very special debt to a group of your wonderful cowboys."

His pronunciation of the word 'cowboys' had an almost comic, yet wonderfully respectful ring to it.

"Because of their courageous actions which I know many of you have read about or seen on television, my homeland and my son were saved from an evil group of people who wanted to do us great harm. My son Rolf and I would like to thank the organizers of this rodeo for giving us the opportunity to publicly recognize this special group of people tonight."

He passed the microphone to Rolf and the familiar, high-pitched voice of the Prince caused C. J. and Josh to grin at one another as it filled the vast Coliseum.

"First of all," the young Prince told the crowd, "I want you to know that I am indebted to Mr. Willy Nelson who gave us the wonderful words 'My Heroes Have Always Been Cowboys'."

Rolf was interrupted by a thunderous cheer from the Coliseum crowd. The story of the Prince and his incredible encounter with Baron Steg had become public within hours of the unscheduled interruption of the polo match. It had been impossible to keep it secret any longer. In fact, Prince Ludwig, when he heard the details, insisted on releasing the complete story to the media and the public. The story had made national celebrities of everyone from the D Lazy D, especially Josh, Jenny, C. J. and Cindy.

When the noise from the crowd died down, Prince Rolf continued, "I would like to ask Mr. and Mrs. Roy

Douglas, Josh and Jenny Douglas, Cindy McKannin, Mr. Ben Bradley, Mr. Len Tucker, Mr. and Mrs. William Findlay and Clayton Findlay, better known as C. J., to come to the centre of the arena please."

It took a few minutes but finally they all made it to the centre of the Coliseum floor. Ben Bradley, Len Tucker, Jenny and Cindy were all on horseback. Roy Douglas came out from behind the chutes while Laura Douglas and the Findlays made their way down from the seats.

C. J. and Josh jumped down from the chute gate they were perched on and sprinted to where the two Princes were standing. As they reached Rolf, each of them grabbed him and danced about in a joyful embrace of long-lost friends. Jenny and Cindy both planted kisses on Rolf's smiling cheek.

When order was restored, Prince Ludwig stepped to the microphone once again.

"As I mentioned, my son and I would like to publicly express our gratitude to these very brave, very kind people.

"At this time I want to extend an invitation to all of you," he gestured to include everyone in the Douglas outfit, "to pay an official visit to Mendenstein next summer to receive the Medal of Valor, the highest honor my government can bestow.

"I should like to point out that never before in the history of Mendenstein has this honor been given to anyone who is not a citizen of our Principality. I am very proud that you will be the first from outside my land to receive these medals. And I thank you from the bottom of my heart. I hope you can accept our invitation."

At that the Prince stepped away from the microphone. Everyone from the D Lazy D turned to look at Roy Douglas, the acknowledged leader of the ranch.

He moved to the microphone. "Your Highness. We want to thank you for your kind words and for the invitation to come to Mendenstein to receive the Medals of Valor.

"I'm not sure that we deserve such high honors for just trying to help out someone we like very much."

Roy paused for a moment. "Just the same," he continued, "I hope you have plenty of room in the bunkhouse because we wouldn't miss this for the world."

At that moment, C. J. threw his hat in the air and Jenny became so excited, she lost her head and actually hugged her brother. Prince Ludwig took the microphone from Roy and said, "Now, let's rodeo!"

Once again, a tumultuous ovation answered his words. Rolf with a wave to his father ran for the chutes with C. J. and Josh.

Though they were flushed with the excitement of Rolf's arrival, the two steer riders knew they would have to hurry to get ready for their event.

"So tell me what's happening," Rolf said as his two friends worked. "Are you doing well here at the Finals?"

"You bet," C. J. told him as he applied a final coat of resin to his gloves. "Josh is winning the Steer Riding.

He practically has the championship in the bag."

"Well, not exactly," Josh corrected him. "I'm winning by thirty-five points but if the guy who is second wins the go-round today he gets forty points. If I don't get any, he wins."

"And guess who is second," C. J. said, the smile disappearing from his face. "None other than Miles Shivers."

"What?" Rolf reacted in disbelief. "Well, that does it, you simply must not lose. You have to beat that... that..."

"It's okay," Josh interrupted him. "I think we know what you're trying to say."

"And what about you, C. J.?" the Prince asked. "How have you done at the Finals?"

"Oh, I've done okay," C. J. replied. "I've ridden all my steers; I just haven't scored high enough. I'm sitting fourth, but I'm satisfied. It's just a heck of a thrill being here."

"Speaking of jerks, as we were a minute ago," Josh interjected, " whatever happened to Baron Steg after High Park?"

"No one knows," Rolf shrugged. "He disappeared, although the police caught most of his men."

"You mean he got away?" C. J. asked in amazement.

"Apparently so," Rolf shook his head disappointedly. "They think he made it out of Canada but the authorities aren't sure where he is now.

"You think he could ever come back and try to take

over Mendenstein again?" Josh asked the Prince.

Rolf shook his head. "My father thinks it'll be a long time before we hear any more from Baron Steg. All of the people who are working with my father now are very loyal to Mendenstein. They are good people who can be trusted," the Prince concluded.

"Well that's good news," Josh responded.

"And what about Jenny and Cindy? How are they doing at the Finals?" Rolf resumed his questions.

"About the same as me," C. J. replied. "They've both placed in a couple of rounds but they don't have a chance of winning the championship."

"They're not disappointed though," Josh noted. "They're the two youngest barrel racers here and they're excited to be a part of all this." He waved an arm to indicate the whole aura of the Finals.

"Yes, I can understand that," Rolf nodded his agreement. "I doubt if I've ever seen a place so full of excitement."

"You know something," C. J. said suddenly to Josh, "I just realized that this will be the last steer ride for you and me."

"Geez, you're right!" Josh exclaimed. "I guess I hadn't really thought about it. Next year we'll be over the age limit."

"Well, in that case cousin, let's make it a good one," he said playfully punching C. J. in the arm. Just then the chute boss yelled that the steers were in and it was time for the riders to start getting their ropes on the animals.

"Good luck guys." Rolf solemnly shook hands with them both.

"Come on," Josh told him, "you can climb up on the chutes where you can see."

Quickly the two riders climbed over the chutes and down onto their steers. Roy Douglas was helping Josh who would be the first of the two boys out. Len Tucker was in the chute with C. J. helping him set his rope.

Of the first three steer riders out, two were bucked off and the third marked 61 points.

As Josh was completing his preparations for his all-important ride, announcer Hank Parker explained the situation to the crowd. "With his 35 point lead, all this cowboy has to do is ride this steer and he will place in the go-round and win the Canadian Championship."

Josh was ready! He nodded his head. The gate opened and he found himself aboard six hundred and fifty pounds of leaping, gyrating fury. Josh was caught by surprise by the power of the steer and was quickly pulled down over the front of the steer.

The steer went high and crashed down again. Josh was pulled forward again. As the steer threw its head back as part of its next move, Josh was struck full in the face by the rank animal.

The blow stunned the rider and he loosened his handhold. In the next second, Josh was catapulted from the steer's back and landed heavily in the Coliseum dirt.

The klaxon sounded a full two seconds later.

The crowd groaned in disappointment and Roy Douglas ran to his fallen son's side.

"Are you okay, Josh?" he asked just as a paramedic arrived to help.

Josh sat up, shook his head and refused the help of the medical man.

"I'm ... all right," he said and stood up on wobbly legs.

Over the microphone, Hank Parker was lamenting the fate of one of his favorite contestants.

"Well folks," the announcer told the crowd, "that buck-off might have cost that young man his chance at the Canadian Steer Riding Championship.

"If Miles Shivers can win this go-round, he'll collect 40 points and be the Champion," Hank explained.

Miles was next. As soon as the steer came out of the chute, it was clear Miles would ride his steer. To make matters worse, he grinned throughout his entire ride. At the sound of the eight-second horn, he stepped confidently off his steer, tossed his hat in the air and yelled "Yeah!" at the top of his lungs.

The judges seemed to agree with Miles' assessment of his performance. They gave him 74 points.

Now only one thing could keep Miles from winning the Championship. Only C. J. Findlay, his archenemy from Ontario, could stop him.

C. J. couldn't win the Championship himself but he *could* win the go-round. If he did that, Miles would drop to second and collect only thirty points in the round, leaving him five behind Josh.

Roy Douglas was now beside C. J. but said nothing about the importance of the ride. Roy knew that C. J. was aware of what it meant if he could score higher than Miles.

Josh reached down and gave his cousin a pat of encouragement on the shoulder. C. J. looked up and could clearly see the shiner forming around Josh's left eye.

C. J. scooted up on his rope, thrust out his chest and took a deep breath.

From the back of the chute, Rolf leaned down and said to him, "Hey, C. J. ... ride for the crown."

"Ride for the Crown!" The words echoed again and again in C. J.'s mind.

He nodded his head and the gate swung open. The steer jumped high and to the right, coming down with a bone-jarring crunch. Up and back down the animal bucked hard, this time to the left. On its third jump, the steer turned back one hundred and eighty degrees and came down facing the chutes.

Then it made a half turn and got higher in the air than on any of the previous jumps. As it landed, C. J. was forced forward just as Josh had been.

He knew he had to get back up or he'd be bucked off. With every ounce of strength he could muster, C. J. forced his body to sit straight up and resist the tremendous downdraft the steer was causing.

Then, as if it knew that it had done everything it could to dislodge this stubborn rider and nothing would work, the steer seemed to ease off. Its last couple of jumps were easier to handle and when the eight seconds were signalled C. J. was squarely in the middle of the steer working his heels into the animal's sides in an effort to gain important points.

He dismounted safely from the steer and arrived back at the chutes out of breath.

Josh was pounding him on the back to congratulate him for his effort and Rolf was dancing up and down excitedly in front of him.

The crowd hadn't stopped cheering and Josh was forced to yell over the noise. "I don't care if you beat him or not. That was one heck of a ride," he shouted.

"Well here it is, we have the results in the Steer Riding," Hank Parker's voice boomed over the roar of the crowd. "C. J. Findlay's score was 76 points.

"C. J. will win today's go-round and that means that the new Canadian Steer Riding Champion is Josh Douglas. Let's salute these two great cowboys."

And as the Coliseum crowd rose for a noisy and prolonged tribute to Josh and C. J., the two boys stepped forward to accept the accolades. Between them was their friend and greatest fan – Rolf.

As they waved to the crowd, Josh leaned over to shake C. J.'s hand. "Like I said, that was a heck of a ride," he said.

"A heck of a 'ride for the crown,' " the Prince of Mendenstein corrected.